Try Me:
Brie's Submission #4

By
Red Phoenix

Try Me: Brie's Submission

Copyright © 2016 by Red Phoenix
Print Edition

RedPhoenix69@live.com

Edited by Amy Parker, Proofed by Becki Wyer & Marilyn Cooper
Cover by CopperLynn
Phoenix symbol by Nicole Delfs

*Previously published as part of *Brie Embraces the Heart of Submission*
Adult Reading Material (18+)

Dedication

As always, I must give love and thanks to MrRed,
the man behind my fantasies.

I also want to thank the many fans who have sent
cards, hand-crafted art, and special gifts.
Your sweet spirits and kind ways have blown me away.
I keep each one I've had the honor to receive,
and I cherish them deeply.

CONTENTS

New Toy

S ir walked into the bedroom nonchalantly, while Brie stumbled over herself as she followed behind him. The knowledge that they were headed to Russia to see the Dom, Rytsar Durov, had her completely discombobulated.

Master commanded her to lie on the bed, her legs spread open for him. She did as he'd asked, watching while he retrieved something from his extensive rack of toys in the back of his closet. Although most Doms displayed their instruments, Sir seemed to enjoy the suspense of his sub not knowing what he would use until the scene was about to begin.

He came out holding up a white device that looked suspiciously like an oversized microphone. Were they going to sing karaoke together? A burst of laughter nearly escaped her lips, but she squelched it.

"I can tell by the amusement on your face that you have no idea what this is," Sir stated.

She nodded, trying to look properly serious.

He held up the device, which had a round head that

tapered into a long handle and a short electrical cord that hung from it. There was nothing sexy or kinky about it. "This is a tool of choice for Durov. I feel you should be familiar with it before we go. There is no doubt in my mind that it will be used while we are there."

Whatever it was, the toy was clunky and unsexy. Brie couldn't imagine why the Russian Dom would prefer it.

Sir stripped before plugging in the toy and joining her on the bed. "It only has two speeds."

He flipped it on and a low rumbling emanated from the toy. *A vibrator…* Her whole body suddenly tensed. *Is that huge thing going inside?*

Sir's laughter filled the room as if she'd voiced her fear aloud. "No, téa. This is an external toy."

Brie relaxed back on the pillow, breathing a sigh of relief. However, she couldn't miss the mischievous glint in his eyes when he ordered, "Open your legs wider."

Now she was nervous.

He announced, "I think the lower one should prove enough for you."

Brie was surprised, considering she always used the highest setting on her little bullet vibrator. A low vibration was just an irritating tease. *Maybe that's part of Sir's evil plan…*

Sir placed it on her clit. It, and all of the surrounding area, rumbled with the low but intense vibration. She moaned softly. It was pleasant.

When he adjusted the angle slightly, her clit instantly became erect and began to quiver. Brie settled farther into the pillow, her back naturally arching in pleasure.

"You like the feel of the Hitachi, do you?"

Brie sighed with satisfaction. "It's very nice, Master."

His eyes got that mischievous look again, causing her concern. "I want you to give in to the orgasm. Don't force it, just let it come naturally."

Her breath quickened. This wasn't going to be a session of orgasm denial, so why was Sir wearing an impish grin?

She closed her eyes and concentrated on the intense, all-encompassing vibration. She mentally embraced the stimulation and Brie could feel the spark burst into flame as the orgasm started to build in her core. It wasn't coming in a rush; no, this was a slow burn that could not be denied because of the sheer size of the toy. Her clit could not escape the teasing vibrations.

Brie opened her eyes and her heart skipped a beat at the lust in her Master's stare. It was obvious he enjoyed bringing her to climax. However, the look held something more she could not define—it made her feel that this was both an act of love for her and dominance over her.

Without any struggle, she reached the edge. "I'm coming, Master," she purred as her hips lifted slightly of their own accord. Sir kept the vibrator directly on her clit throughout her climax, making it almost too intense.

When it ended she melted onto the bed, but only momentarily, for Master was not finished. His wicked grin widened when she started to whimper.

Brie's freshly-come pussy could not handle the intense stimulation of the vibrator now. "Please, Master. Too much."

"I command you to take it," he stated.

Brie squirmed under the vibrator, but there was no escaping the giant head. Her clit burned in protest and she instinctively moved away, but Sir's hand landed on her pelvis.

"Stop moving."

When Brie became still, he lifted his hand from her. However, the intensity of the vibration was driving her insane and she protested again, "Too much, too much!"

Sir leaned forward and said in a husky whisper, "Harness that feeling and come for me."

Brie's bottom lip quivered. How could she? It was so concentrated it was almost painful. Thankfully, the lesson of the beam came to her. During her session with the violet wand, Sir had instructed her to hold onto a pole. If the stimulation became too much, all she had to do was let go. Having that level of control had helped her tolerate more intense stimulation.

This situation was similar in that Sir was giving her a level of control again. He was not holding her down; Master had commanded she remain motionless of her own will.

With great effort, Brie stopped fighting the vibration. She willed her body to relax and give in to the stimulation, to embrace it. Slowly, her muscles obeyed and the vibration went from painful to wanted. She arched her back and pressed herself into the toy.

"Good girl," he murmured.

Brie let out a loud whimper as the second, far stronger orgasm took hold of her body and wrung her out with its powerful contractions. She was trembling afterwards, still writhing from the merciless vibration.

Her eyes began watering. "Please, Master! No more…"

"One more, téa."

She groaned in protest, but mentally accepted his command. Brie closed her eyes and calmed her feeling of panic. *One more… Sir is asking for only one more.* Brie slowed her breathing until it was deep and even. Once she was calm, she could better concentrate on the intense fire between her legs.

Having already come twice in rapid succession, it did not take her long to urge the third once she'd embraced it. The final orgasm felt like an exorcism when it struck. Her thighs began shaking violently. She screamed when Sir slipped his finger into her pussy and her muscles repeatedly clamped around him when she climaxed. This one went on forever, ebbing and then returning with a vengeance as the vibrator rumbled on.

Finally, the toy was lifted off her clit and she melted into the pillow, tears in her eyes. Brie never knew orgasms could be like that—extreme, but equally torturous.

Sir turned it off and put the device down. "God, you are beautiful when you come like that."

She slowly turned her head towards him, every movement an effort.

He swept away a strand of her sweat-drenched hair. "Impressive, téa."

Her body so wrung out that even talking was difficult, Brie whispered, "What is that thing called, Master?"

He smirked. "A Magic Wand."

She snorted and looked up at the ceiling. "More like

a Merciless Wand."

"If it's merciless you want, it's merciless you shall have."

Before Brie could voice a protest, Sir moved between her legs and thrust his hard cock into her. She cried out as he began fucking her over-stimulated pussy.

"You are hot like fire, woman!"

Brie's clit was still buzzing from the vibrator, and his forceful thrusts just added to the dizzying effect.

"I'm going to come, and come hard," her Master proclaimed.

Her screams were more like whimpers as he revved up for the final act. The sound of their sex was enticingly juicy because of how wet and excited she was.

"Master, I..." she began, but lost all train of thought as he pounded his cock into her like a jackhammer. Only three words followed: "Oh...my...God!"

He grunted like a ravenous lion as he gave in to his desire, pumping his seed deep within her. Master pressed up against her sex with the last thrust and her pussy gave its final encore, a fluttering climax to milk his cock.

Sir kissed a tear that remained on her cheek. "And that, my dear, concludes your introduction to the Magic Wand."

A Little Dish on Clark

Brie held up her philosophy textbook from college. "Why do I still have this? I'll never use it."

Lea giggled. "Give it to charity. I'm sure some poor college student would appreciate not spending a hundred bucks for the book."

Brie turned it over and looked at the price tag. "A hundred and eighteen bucks, girl." She flipped through the pages. "I think I cracked it open maybe...um...three times. The teacher didn't like teaching from books." She tossed it in the 'give away' pile and dug back into the box.

Lea had volunteered to help Brie move in to Sir's apartment. However, Sir had suggested the two first sort through the boxes, dividing them into three piles: 'keep', 'toss', and 'give away'. It was proving to be a daunting task.

Lea held up several DVDs. "What are these?"

Brie broke out into a grin. "That is my documentary, missy. I like to keep it on as many different formats as I can so there's no chance of losing it." She dug into her pocket. "Here it is on my USB drive."

"What? You keep it with you all the time?" Lea asked in amazement.

"Not normally." She laughed. "But Sir wants me to start working on it again." She looked around guiltily. "I know we should be working, but you wanna take a peek at what I have so far?"

Lea nodded vigorously.

Brie grabbed her computer and the two sat on boxes as she loaded it up. "I've been working on the first time you came to my apartment. Do you remember that night, after our first auction?"

"Oh, Master Harris! He was so damn sexy in his doctor getup and with all those naughty instruments…"

"Yeah, you pretty much were crushing on him that night."

Brie hit play and the two started giggling as they listened to their detailed summaries of the day-long auctions.

"We were such newbies then," Brie snickered. She pointed to her face in the video. "See, that's me, trying not to look totally freaked out when you talk about him inserting the instruments."

Lea leaned in to take a closer look, and burst out laughing. "I had no idea. I thought you shared my lust for the man."

"No, I thought you were nuts to want to play 'doctor' with anyone."

Lea sat back. "Well, that's funny, since you spent time with Master Harris yourself, and if I recall right, you loved it."

"*Doctor* Harris was nice, but he couldn't compare to Rytsar."

Lea shifted uneasily, causing Brie to wonder if her girlfriend still had a major crush on the doctor.

Lea lifted her hands up to her face and batted her eyes, imitating Brie's excitement from that night. "Just look at the way you're glowing as you talk about the Russian. I thought for sure you had fallen in love with the Dom, the way you were gushing."

Brie hit pause on the computer. "Well, I admit I definitely had a crush on Rytsar." She smiled self-consciously. "I actually cried when the night was over."

Lea burst into giggles. "That's my stinky cheese, falling for every man she scenes with."

"Like you're any better! Remember how sad you were when Master Harris sent me an apple?"

Lea rolled her eyes. "You already had the handsome Russian *and* Tono. As if you needed another man on your chastity belt."

Brie bumped her shoulder. "I still think you and Master Harris would make a fine pair, you know."

She looked at Brie coyly. "Oh, we have enjoyed a few scenes since…"

"No!"

Lea giggled again. "Don't try collaring me with the man, girlfriend. I'm enjoying myself too much right now. So many directions I could go—I can't decide."

Brie decided to ask the question that she'd been longing to ask for weeks. "What about Ms. Clark?"

Darn, if Lea hadn't turned bright pink all over.

"Spill the beans, girl!" Brie demanded.

Lea looked positively love-struck when she answered. "We haven't actually scened together since graduation, but she's taken me to a couple of clubs. Let's just say, I think there's a deeper connection brewing between us."

The thought of dating Ms. Clark made Brie shiver—and not in a good way. "So, have you learned anything more about her?"

Lea's voice dropped down to a whisper. "I think she has a thing for the Russian."

Brie was so shocked, she blurted, "What?!"

"Shh… I'm only telling you because you're my best friend."

Brie shook her head to clear it. "OMG, things are suddenly making sense. That's why she was so weird when he won me at the auction…and it explains her strange reaction when he rated me higher than she expected." She giggled into her hand. "Mistress Clark and Rytsar? I can't even picture it."

"Well, apparently neither can the Russian. Poor Mistress Clark is suffering from unrequited love."

"But…*Ms. Clark*? Is she even capable of submitting to someone else?"

Lea shrugged. "Guess it just takes the right individual."

The revelation put the Domme in a whole new light. Ms. Clark was looking for love—no different than the rest of humanity. She'd just managed to hide it under an exterior of impenetrable force.

"I always thought she was of the 'female' persuasion," Brie protested.

"Oh, no, I have seen her with male submissives. God, she is sexy when she subdues them."

"Really?"

"Yeah, that woman is multitalented. You don't know this, but she has many admirers. Unfortunately, the only one she really desires is the one who turned her down."

"What? Rytsar knows how she feels?"

"Yeah. From what I gather, Sir was somehow involved. Whatever happened, she ended up very hurt and resentful."

"It's a wonder she still works at the Center."

Lea gave her a sad smile. "I think Mistress Clark holds out hope the Russian will change his mind, and she wants to be here when he does. I can't tell you how unhappy she was when Sir quit, as he's her only link to Rytsar."

Brie shook her head slowly, unable to process this new side to the female trainer. "How is it that a dominant personality could think that way?"

"Love does strange things to people," Lea answered. "But I tell you this, if I could take Ms. Clark's pain away, I would."

Brie looked at her friend, understanding the deeper meaning behind the statement. "So are you telling me that you're in love with her?"

Lea tilted her head and looked at Brie with a solemn expression. "At this point I'm not sure if I can distinguish between love and lust. All I know is that the world is a much better place when I'm around her. She makes me feel alive like no one else, not even the doctor."

A random thought flashed through Brie's head.

"Does that mean you're jealous of Rytsar?"

Lea became flustered, which was so uncharacteristic of her. "I… Hmm… Good question. I'll have to get back to you on that."

Ms. Clark in love with Rytsar…what a tangled mess!

"Brie."

She nearly jumped out of her skin when she saw Sir in the doorway. How long had he been standing there? Brie stood up and addressed him. "Yes, Sir?"

"There has been a change of plans. Marquis just called, claiming Celestia is in dire need of company. He said she's been lonely since returning home from the hospital. We'll be leaving in an hour." He looked at her laptop sitting on the box. "Finish what you can and reschedule for a later date."

Brie felt guilty, knowing she had wasted time gossiping with Lea when she should have been unpacking. "We will, Sir."

"Lea."

Her friend looked up at Sir with a guilty expression, as if she had failed him too.

"I am glad you came today. Brie never laughs as much as when she is with you."

He left them without any reprimand.

"That was so sweet of him to say," Lea cooed.

"My Master is a good man."

"The best!"

Brie put her computer away and the two made quick work of three more boxes before Lea had to leave. Sir escorted them both out, giving Brie the meal he had cooked for Celestia while the girls had finished their work. Whatever it was, it smelled delicious—far beyond anything Brie could have prepared.

"Thank you, Sir Davis. You really didn't have to make me a meal, but thanks," Lea joked, grabbing the meal from Brie.

Sir shook his head good-naturedly as he took it back. "Watch yourself, Lea."

Brie was amazed at Lea's boldness. Not too many people were brave enough to joke with Sir. It made her love Lea all the more. "Call you tomorrow?"

Lea gave her a big hug. "I'm counting on it, subbie."

On the drive there, Sir surprised Brie by stating, "Although I have made dinner, there is something I want you to cook especially for Marquis Gray once we get there."

She hid her disappointment with a smile. Having to cook for Marquis was humiliating, especially after the egg fiasco just before graduation. "Yes, Sir."

He winked at her. "I know he will appreciate it."

She wondered about this sudden trip to visit them and asked, "Is everything okay with Celestia, Sir? Is she having trouble recovering from her emergency appendectomy?"

He chuckled. "She is well enough. I think this is more for Marquis' sake. He has been at home taking care of his sub for more than a week, and I think it is driving him mad."

Brie was struck again by the paradigm shift—first

with Ms. Clark and now with Marquis. She had always imagined him to be almost Zen-like in his approach to life. The idea that Marquis was going stir-crazy seemed so…human.

"I couldn't help over hearing part of your conversation with Lea," Sir stated. "During our stay in Russia, Ms. Clark's name is not to be mentioned."

Brie couldn't imagine what had happened to provoke such a command.

"I won't, Sir."

"I personally don't care for gossip, but in this case it was beneficial. You needed to be aware of that dynamic so you would not mistakenly mention it. Although the incident occurred years ago, there are still raw nerves on all sides."

"May I ask what happened, Sir?"

"You may ask, but I will not answer. It is a private matter."

Brie cringed, feeling bad for prying. Humbled, she assured him, "I will not ask again, Sir. Please forgive me."

"Lea is a natural gossip. I know that is not your nature."

She didn't want Sir to think badly of Lea. "I promise we will work hard next time to make up for today."

"See that you do," he replied as they pulled into the driveway of a sprawling, ranch-style home. He added, almost as an afterthought, "It would be nice to be settled, Brie. I've never been a fan of boxes."

Sir's comment warmed her heart. It was his way of saying that he wanted her there permanently. She blurted, "I love you, Sir!"

His devastating smile set her heart aflutter as she got out of the car, but those feelings of momentary bliss disappeared as soon as she stood on Marquis Gray's doorstep.

I'm a Condor

Sir rang the doorbell and told Brie to stop fidgeting. "You will do fine," he promised, just as the door opened.

Brie tensed when she saw Marquis Gray. It had only been a couple of weeks, but she had forgotten what a commanding presence he had until those dark eyes greeted her. She quickly looked down, not wanting to be reprimanded.

"Well, isn't this a nice surprise?"

"I doubt you could call it a surprise when you demanded we come," Sir replied with a smirk.

"No need to speak of it to Celestia. I wouldn't want her to feel she was a burden to anyone."

"I suspect she is not the problem," Sir murmured as he held up the dish he'd prepared. "This is for later. My sub is going to make you an appetizer first."

Through hooded eyes, she watched Marquis for his reaction. She did not miss the look of revulsion that flitted across his face. "How kind of you."

She wasn't sure if he was speaking to Sir or to her, so

she kept her head down. She was determined not to fail him—or Sir.

"But first, you two really must see Celestia. She has been cooped up here since I brought her home from the hospital after the surgery, and she is in dire need of company."

Brie followed Sir as Marquis led them through the house. It looked like the model homes one saw in magazines. Tall, vaulted ceilings, an expansive fireplace, tons of perfectly placed knick-knacks. Not what she had imagined for Marquis at all. It made her wonder if Celestia had been the decorator. If so, she was quite talented. The place maintained a homey and inviting feel, despite its perfection.

Marquis took them to the great room. It was equally impressive, with its wall of books, large screen TV, and huge bay window. The room had it all, including a smiling Celestia, who was lying on the couch.

"May I, Sir?" Brie asked.

"Of course."

She walked to Celestia's side and knelt beside her, grabbing her hand. "How are you? I was so scared when I heard what had happened!"

Celestia's angelic voice was as pure as Brie remembered. "I am doing well, Miss Bennett. Marquis is overly protective of his sub. He won't let me do anything while I recover."

"Doctor's orders," Marquis corrected.

Celestia smiled up at her Master. "You take good care of me." He offered his hand and she kissed it tenderly.

It was sweet. The two had a special bond Brie adored.

"It is good to hear you are well, Celestia," Sir said kindly. "You are greatly admired and your bad health was a distress to us all."

Celestia bowed her head. "That's very kind of you to say, Sir Davis."

"Miss Bennett," Marquis said, "I hear you have had issues with Mr. Wallace since the collaring ceremony."

She looked at him warily, only nodding when she glanced into his perilous eyes. They penetrated her to the core.

"I've spoken to him once and we will be meeting with him as a panel while you are in Russia. He is in significant need of direction. However, I can't help but wonder what you feel for the young Dom."

She looked to Sir before she spoke. He nodded, so she answered Marquis openly. "I care about Mr. Wallace, but only as a friend."

"That must stop."

She looked at him in shock. She was about to protest, but remembered his position and asked respectfully, "May I ask why, Marquis Gray?"

"He cannot distinguish the difference. He is convinced you feel the same and will not be able to move forward if he continues to receive mixed signals from you."

Sir put his hand on Brie's shoulder, stating, "I've already told her what to do if she encounters him again."

"I am not talking about that, Sir Davis. I am talking about her private thoughts. I personally believe those connections are equally potent. Even the simple act of dwelling on Mr. Wallace continues a link that needs to be severed. Until he is in control of his emotions, you should banish all thoughts of him."

Brie thought Marquis was being overdramatic, but then she thought back to the many times she had fantasized about Sir during her training. She'd felt a very real connection to him then, and look at them now…

She glanced at Sir, not wanting to commit to anything he did not agree with.

Sir addressed Marquis. "Although I doubt Brie will have any thoughts of the boy while we are in Russia, I believe it is a valid point."

Brie nodded to Marquis. "Then I will sever my thoughts, Marquis Gray. I don't want him to hurt anymore. Faelan deserves a fresh start."

"Fine." Marquis looked down at Celestia lovingly. "I believe my sub is due for some sustenance."

Sir inquired, "May we have free rein of your kitchen?"

"Certainly."

Sir guided Brie into the immaculate kitchen. He looked through the refrigerator before giving her directions. "It looks like you have all the necessary ingredients." He shut the refrigerator door and faced her. "I want you to create the best damn omelet he's ever eaten."

Brie felt her stomach sink to the ground. Her worst nightmare! *Cooking an omelet for Marquis?* "Only if it pleases you, Sir," she replied, stating her reluctance respectfully.

He chuckled. "It pleases me."

Her sigh was heavy when he left the kitchen. *An omelet for Marquis… Oh, the humanity!*

Brie gathered the needed ingredients, including his favorites: green onion, bacon, and Swiss. She counted out the eggs and noted there were only enough to make three omelets. She hoped it would be unnecessary to use them all.

While the others talked in the adjacent room, Brie set to work. There was a sense of excitement, despite the fear. She knew how to cook this omelet and if Sir wasn't willing to partake of her skills, at least Marquis could.

It only took two tries to make a perfect omelet. Sir had provided a covered plate so that she could properly display it. With pride, she placed the silver lid over it and walked into the room to join the group, the plate held proudly in both hands.

"Ah, you look as if you have created a masterpiece," Marquis complimented as he sat down on the couch next to Celestia.

"I could not have done it without your patience, Marquis Gray. I am grateful," she said with a bow as she placed it on the coffee table, along with a fork and napkin.

"I am anxious to try it."

Everyone watched as he lifted the lid—Celestia with her pleasant smile and Sir with a playful smirk. Brie bit her lip in anticipation.

The look on Marquis' face would have been comical if she hadn't been the one to make the dish. "Oh, no…" He quickly slammed the lid back down and closed his eyes.

The room was silent.

He said, in a voice of forced calm, "Miss Bennett, I appreciate the effort you put into the dish. However, after our last session in the kitchen I have sworn off omelets forever."

Sir put his hand over his mouth to hide his snicker. Celestia, on the other hand, took pity on Brie. "I would love to sample your work."

With much effort, Marquis took off the lid again and cut a small piece for her. He lifted the fork to her lips and turned away as she chewed.

"It's simply lovely, Miss Bennett. So light and fluffy. Thank you."

Brie bowed. "My pleasure, Celestia."

"Whose idea was it to cook the omelet tonight?" Marquis asked as he cut another piece for Celestia.

Brie said nothing.

"I see." Marquis turned to Sir. "Your idea of a joke, Sir Davis? It wasn't enough to put me in charge of the cooking unit last session, I take it."

Sir bit back his amusement. "I wanted you to enjoy the benefits of your labor, Gray. It was only fair. You know how I detest eggs. The whole Center smelled of them for a week."

Marquis actually smiled then. "You have an overly sensitive nose, Sir Davis." He raised his eyebrow and stated, "Surely you're not suggesting I chose that particular dish with you in mind?"

"That is exactly what I'm suggesting."

He chuckled. "Unfortunately, I ended up punishing

us both." He gave Celestia another bite before addressing Brie. "Although the sight of this dish nauseates me, I must compliment you on the work. I can tell it has the right texture, and apparently you remembered what I prefer in an omelet. Kudos, Miss Bennett." His praise gave her an unexpected thrill. "And…" he lifted the fork to Celestia's lips again, "my sub seems to enjoy the flavor. A job well done. How many tries did it take?"

Brie said proudly, "Two."

"A vast improvement indeed. There is hope for you yet."

"Thank you, Marquis Gray."

Sir spoke up, "Unfortunately, we must cut this visit short. Brie and I both have work to do tonight, but I have your meal warming in the oven."

"It was lovely of you to come, Sir Davis. Miss Bennett," Celestia said, trying to get up.

Marquis gently pushed her back on the couch. "Stay still," he chided. "I'll see them out."

As they walked to the front of the house, Marquis told Sir, "To be honest, I questioned whether you would be a good match for Miss Bennett, despite her infatuation with you. Especially when I heard the reports of her interactions with Mr. Wallace afterwards. However, tonight those concerns have been silenced. I see a peace in her eyes I have not seen before."

Brie's heart nearly burst with joy when she heard his observation.

"It is good to hear you acknowledge that fact," Sir replied. "I did not make the decision lightly, nor did I do it solely for my own benefit."

"Understood," Marquis answered. "But one had to question your intentions, based on your previous actions."

"What one might label as a 'breach of protocol', another might see as a fated encounter," Sir responded.

Marquis shook his head as he opened the door. "Regardless of whether I agree with you or not, I wish you both safe travels. Miss Bennett, I hope you will visit again soon. I am sure my sub will enjoy your tales of Russia."

"Thank you, Marquis Gray. Please tell Celestia how happy I am to see her looking so well."

"I shall. The same can be said for us. It is good to see you thriving, Miss Bennett."

The drive home was agreeably quiet. Sir seemed as satisfied by the night's events as she was. It pleased Brie that he had openly acknowledged his feelings for her in front of Marquis. Although Sir hadn't used the 'L' word, the meaning was the same. She assumed it was a big step for him.

The night still had one pleasant surprise left. After they returned to the apartment, Sir told her to work on editing her film while he polished a presentation he was to give the next day.

They sat on the couch beside each other with their computers. It was so pleasant and sweet that Brie decided to google something she'd been curious about. Sir had once told her that he was a condor, and said it with such tenderness that she knew it held significance to him. She typed in the word 'condor'.

Brie glanced over the stats of the bird, noting that

she had been right. They were a type of vulture—not sexy in the least. However, the California condor was the largest bird in North America. It wasn't until she got to the behavior of the creature that she finally grasped Sir's meaning. She was surprised to learn the birds lived to be incredibly old—like fifty to sixty years—and the males waited until they were sexually mature before picking a female. Her heart skipped a beat when she read the words, 'condors mate for life'. That was what he'd meant!

'I'm a condor' had to be the most romantic thing she'd ever heard.

She glanced at Sir, hardly able to contain her joy.

He looked up from his screen and smiled. "What?"

"You're a condor, Sir."

He raised his eyebrow. "Yes, I am."

She smiled shyly. "I'm a condor, too."

Her Parents

B rie was grateful to finish out her last day at the tobacco shop. Her boss had given the two new employees the day off so that it was just like old times— just the two of them. Although it was bittersweet to leave Mr. Reynolds behind, she couldn't wait to be free of the place. It was *so* mind-numbingly boring compared to the life she was leading now.

At the end of the day, Mr. Reynolds handed her a small gift.

"What's this?" she asked, both surprised and touched.

"A little remembrance. It has been a pleasure working with you, Brie. You will be sorely missed around here. My only consolation is that I will see you on an odd holiday or two."

"What? Don't you get together with your nephew more often than that?"

"No. He's a busy man. I understand."

She smiled brightly. "I'll see if I can change that."

"Open it," Mr. Reynolds encouraged.

Brie carefully unwrapped the pretty paper. She lifted the lid and smiled as she took the gift out of the box. It was a keychain with a tiny pack of Treasurer cigarettes hanging from it. The very cigarettes Sir had asked for the first night they'd met in the shop. "Mr. Reynolds, how did you know?"

"Thane was surprisingly open when he asked about the cute little cashier at my shop. He knew very well we don't carry those pricey cigarettes here."

Brie held it up to admire. "I will *treasure* this always," she said with a giggle, giving him a hug. "Truly, it means a lot to me. This little shop is where Sir and I met, where my life really began. Every time I look at it I will smile and think of you."

"I'm glad you like it, Brie." He discreetly wiped a tear from his eye, shaking his head. "This shop won't be the same without you."

She gave Mr. Reynolds another hug. It was hard saying goodbye to the man who'd been a father figure to her since she'd moved to California. She smiled at him sadly, knowing she wouldn't see him on a daily basis after this.

He shook the melancholy look from his face. "So, enjoy yourself in Russia. Be sure to take pics, but only show me the ones you can post publicly," he joked.

It was still weird having Mr. Reynolds aware of her alternative lifestyle, but it was comforting too. He was the only person outside the BDSM community who knew about it—well, besides his wife.

She pulled her keys from her purse and placed them on the new keychain. "There—now you'll be with me wherever I go."

Brie gave him a final kiss on the cheek before heading out of the door. She turned around as she walked away from the small, brick building. "Bye, tobacco shop. It's been real and it's been fun, but I can't say it's been real fun." She snickered to herself as she jumped in her car.

Her new life had officially begun, and tomorrow she was heading off to Russia. But first, Sir had to meet her parents.

Brie was a jumble of nerves as they drove up to her parents' Nebraskan home. She had a bad feeling about the visit, but Sir would not be swayed. She stared out of the window of the rental car, looking at the old place. She'd spent her teenage years here in the small, two-story house on the corner lot, with her devoted but overprotective parents.

"I always hated bringing my boyfriends home to meet my parents," she mumbled, "especially my dad, Sir."

"Is there a point to telling me this?" Sir asked, a hint of humor in his voice.

"Dad would rather I set my sights on my career than waste my potential by getting involved with someone, Sir."

"Understandable…" He got out of the car and opened the door for her.

She took his hand hesitantly. "They're not exactly open-minded either."

"You have mentioned that before, Brie. We're only sharing our status as a couple," he reminded her gently as they walked up to the house.

Brie looked up at her Master as they stood on the front porch—strong, chiseled features, with a decidedly mature appearance. She was afraid his age would be an issue for them, but hoped her parents could see past it.

She closed her eyes, trying to quiet her nerves as Sir reached over and rang the doorbell. It seemed like forever before she heard the unlocking of the latch and the door finally swung open. Her mother, a short, rotund woman with bright green eyes, greeted them with a smile that quickly turned to a concerned frown as she looked Sir over.

"Hey, Mom!" Brie gave her a quick hug to ease the tension. "This is my boyfriend, Thane Davis. Thane, this is my mom, Marcy Bennett."

Sir held out his hand and smiled. "It is an honor to meet you, Mrs. Bennett."

Her mother took his hand and blushed as she shook it. Brie could see it in her mom's eyes—that glimmer of attraction towards the commanding Dom—but it disappeared as soon as her father entered the picture.

"What is your name, sir?" her father asked, in a voice already laced with judgment.

Despite the uncomfortable moment, Brie burst out in a nervous giggle. *Sir...*

Her dad glowered at her before addressing Sir again. "Well?"

"My name is Thane Davis, Mr. Bennett." He held out his hand. "It's a pleasure to meet you."

Her father looked at Sir's offered hand with disdain before engaging him. "I am a frank man, Mr. Davis."

"I find frank talk refreshing," Sir replied.

"What the hell is a man my age doing with my little girl?"

Sir seemed untroubled and asked, "Wouldn't it be best to discuss this inside?"

Brie's mother scanned the neighborhood, as if suddenly afraid the whole world could hear them. She stammered, "Oh! Yes... Come in, come in," gesturing them into the house frantically.

Sir put his hand on the small of Brie's back as he guided her forward. It helped to calm her already frayed nerves. This was not starting off well...

They sat down in the front room, the unused room reserved only for company. Brie's first instinct was to kneel at Sir's feet, feeling in need of his comfort. Instead, she sat beside him.

Her parents sat opposite them with disparaging looks on their faces.

Sir responded to her dad's question. "Actually, there is only an eleven-year difference between us, Mr. Bennett."

"Only?" He turned to Brie. "You never mentioned you were dating an older man, daughter."

Brie bowed her head in shame, knowing now it had been a mistake. "Dad, I love Thane. I didn't mention his age because I wanted you and Mom to meet him in person. I was sure once you met him, you would see what an exceptional person he is."

Her mother frowned again. "We did not send you to California so some 'producer' could turn your head with promises of fame."

Brie shook her head, mortified at her accusation that he was a lecher. "Mom—"

Sir put his hand on Brie's knee and smiled. "I assure you that my intentions are honorable...and," he added drolly, "I am no producer."

"Don't tell me you want to marry her!" her father retorted.

Brie blushed a deep shade of red. Marriage had never been discussed and it was embarrassing that her father was bringing it up now.

She was grateful when Sir answered him with unrattled calm. "No. However, you should know that I care deeply for your daughter."

Her dad laughed. "Oh, I can just imagine how deep your feelings are for my little girl."

Brie squeaked, "Dad! It's not that way at all! We love each other."

His smile was patronizing. "Brie, I believe you have fallen in love with this shyster, but I don't believe for a second your feelings are returned. He wants only one thing from you."

Brie covered her face with her hands. It was dreadful to have Sir treated with such brazen disrespect by her parents. She wanted to curl up and die.

Sir's voice remained reasonable. "If it were as you say, would I be here meeting you in person?"

"I think you came hoping to throw the wool over

our eyes, but we aren't twenty-two like Brianna."

Sir sat farther back on the mauve couch, a subtle show of confidence in an uncomfortable situation. "I'm sure you agree that this visit was necessary. I'm in a serious relationship with your daughter and came to meet you out of respect for your position as Brie's parents."

"Is that right?" Brie's father asked sarcastically. He turned to Brie and demanded, "Have you been over to meet *his* parents?"

Brie gasped and then looked down, shaking her head. Oh, how she didn't want to go there—not *now*!

"My father is dead and my mother left when I was fifteen. We have been estranged ever since."

Brie's mother's expression instantly changed. "Oh…I am so terribly sorry."

But leave it to her father to go right for the jugular. "How did he die, Mr. Davis?"

Sir did not hesitate. "Suicide."

His answer had Brie's mother wringing her hands and saying repeatedly, "I'm so, so sorry…"

However, Brie's father had the opposite reaction. "That alone makes you unsuitable for our only child. Your father was unstable. I do not want an emotionally weak man to have anything to do with my daughter."

Brie could not remain quiet any longer, horrified by her father's callous response. "Dad! Thane's father was a famous violinist who suffered a tragic death. What a terrible thing to say."

Her mother gasped. "Not Alonzo Davis, the musician who killed himself after—?"

Sir interrupted, his voice devoid of emotion. "Yes, Alonzo was my father."

For once, Brie's dad remained silent. It seemed her mother couldn't stand the suffocating hush, so she popped out of her seat. "Let me get us some tea. Everyone likes tea, right?" She disappeared into the kitchen before anyone could answer.

It broke Brie's heart that Sir had wanted to meet her parents, but all they had done was put him down from the moment they'd opened the door. "Should we go, Thane?" she asked, feeling desperate to run.

"No," he replied, squeezing her knee reassuringly.

The room stayed uncomfortably silent until her mother returned with the iced tea. She poured everyone a glass and sat down, asking in an overly pleasant tone, "So, how did you two meet?"

Sir was kind enough to humor her. "I met Brie at the tobacco shop where she worked."

Her father instantly picked up on that. "Worked?" He looked at Brie with concern. "Don't you work there anymore?"

"No, Dad. Yesterday was my last day. Thane wants me working on the documentary I mentioned. The one the well-known producer has shown interest in."

Her mom piped up, "Oh, you mean the documentary about your girlfriends learning the ropes in Hollywood?"

Brie struggled not to snicker. *Learning the ropes...*

Sir stated proudly, "Your daughter has real talent as a filmmaker. I asked her to quit so that she can devote her time solely to the project."

Brie's father's eyes narrowed. "What? Are you supporting my daughter now? Paying her rent?"

"We're living together," Brie corrected.

"Are you, now?" her father said, looking straight at Sir.

"We are in a committed relationship," Sir replied smoothly.

"What kind of child have I raised?" her mother lamented. "You barely know this man and you're already living with him?"

Sir's reply was quick and to the point. "What kind of daughter have you raised? You have raised an intelligent, talented woman, one who is respected and cherished by those who know her. Simply put, you have raised a beautiful person, both inside and out."

Brie blushed under the unreserved praise of her Master.

Her parents were left speechless. Finally, her father cleared his throat. "Yes, we agree that Brie is an exceptional woman, but she is still young. I don't like the idea of her being fettered in a relationship."

Brie wanted to giggle. *Fettered…* Her father's choice of words was perfect.

"I will say it again. I care deeply for your daughter."

"I don't trust you," her father shot back. "After what happened between your parents, I don't see how you could be anything but a philanderer or an utter control freak. Either way, neither is healthy for my daughter."

Sir didn't seem intimidated in the least. "Although I do admit to a need for a certain level of control, I too want what's best for Brie. If it turns out I am not what she needs, I'll willingly step aside."

Brie's father made a grunting sound as he sat back in his chair, digesting Sir's words.

Her mother pleaded with her, "Brie, honey, why the rush? I don't understand how you can go from just meeting each other to living together. Give it time; give yourself a little space before you commit yourself to something like that."

Her dad looked at Sir suspiciously. "Why did you really come today, Mr. Davis?"

"I plan to take your daughter out of the country. We are headed to Russia and I felt it was important for all of us to meet."

"What?!" Her dad turned to her mother, a look of sheer disgust on his face. He turned back to Sir. "Just because your father was rich and famous does not give you the right to do whatever you want or..." he looked directly at Brie, "take whatever you want."

Brie couldn't stay quiet any longer. "Dad, this isn't a case of me asking your permission to go to Russia. We came today so you could meet the man I love. That's it. I don't need your permission for anything. I'm twenty-two, remember?"

He stood up, fuming. "Do you know how stupid that sounds? Twenty-two. You're still just a kid!"

She closed her eyes, collecting herself before replying, "I'm an adult, whether you want to face that fact or not."

"You're not an adult!" her father answered emphatically.

Her mom moved over to her father, putting a hand

on his shoulder. "Bill, we need to be reasonable here. Brie could have kept us in the dark and taken off to God knows where." Her eyes started to tear up. "She's all we have. I couldn't bear not knowing where she is."

"My point exactly," Sir stated.

Brie's father snarled at him, "You do not have permission to take her, Mr. Davis."

Sir nodded his understanding but answered calmly, "Then I leave the decision to your daughter."

It was time to change the traditional dynamics of child and parent. Her parents needed to see her as an adult, free to make her own decisions—and her own mistakes. "I respect you both, but I am choosing to go with Thane to Russia. Either you can accept my decision…or not."

Her father wouldn't even look Sir in the eye when he spoke. "I do not approve of you, Mr. Davis. However, it is obvious I have no influence over my daughter so I will do as she says and accept it, but do not think for one second I am happy about this."

"I will take good care of her."

Her father snorted in disgust.

"Don't you dare let anything happen to our Brie, Mr. Davis," her mother added. She grabbed her daughter in a death grip. "I've missed you so much, Brie darling! We never talk anymore…and now this."

Her father said gruffly, "If anything should happen—anything at all—little girl, you call me and I will be on the next flight out to get you."

"You don't have to worry, Dad," she said, reaching out to give her father a hug. He moved out of her reach, making his feelings painfully clear.

"It will be unnecessary to come for her, Mr. Bennett." Sir said, getting up and pulling a card from his breast pocket. He held it out to the man. "But if you wish to speak to her, this is the number to reach both of us. Keep in mind the time difference and the fact we will be out sightseeing much of the day and into the night."

Her father refused to take the card.

Her mom let go of Brie to take it from Sir. "Thank you." She added apologetically, "I am truly sorry about what happened to your family."

Brie saw it even if her mother did not—that brief flicker of pain before Sir replied. "It was an unfortunate situation but life moves on, as it should."

"Yes," her mom agreed, patting him hesitantly on the shoulder.

Sir smiled kindly. "It was nice to meet you, Mrs. Bennett." He looked over to her father. "To meet you both." Then he glanced at Brie. "Shall we?"

Her mother waved as they walked out to the car, but her father just stared at Brie with an expressionless face. It was terrible to feel this new and unwelcome barrier between them, but she knew Sir had been right to insist on meeting her parents. It was better to be upfront than to hide like a child.

When they were back in the car, Brie looked at Sir sadly. "My parents were awful to you."

"If they had reacted any different, I would have been concerned. They love you and want to protect you. That is a healthy response, in my estimation."

Brie leaned over and kissed him on the cheek.

"You're a good man, Sir."

He chuckled lightly. "And now that we have that over, our trip can begin. I hope you're ready, little sub." His smirk made the butterflies start again.

Oh, Master...

Sir's Past

W hen they boarded the overseas jet, Brie's mouth
fell open. She had never been on a plane so
humongous before. Sir escorted her to a first class seat.
She giggled as she went to sit down. She had never
thought she'd fly first class—ever.

On the seat she found a blanket, an eye mask, slip-
pers and even premium bottled water. She gathered all of
them in her arms and smiled at Sir. "I feel so special."

He chuckled. "You're easily satisfied."

Sir stuffed his items in the seat pocket in front of
him. Brie followed suit. Then she started playing with the
button on her chair. Instead of the seat only going back a
fraction of an inch, this one kept going and going until
she was practically lying down. She giggled at Sir. "It's
like a bed!"

He had an amused look on his face. "You might
want to put that up, Brie. People are still boarding the
plane."

She immediately adjusted the seat back and looked
out of the window at the workers below. They were busy

loading the last of the luggage. "I can't believe I'm going to another country, Sir."

"I am sure this will be the first of many trips. I suspect you'll be traveling often when you're filming."

She turned to him, filled with gratitude. "You think I'll succeed, don't you?"

"I never had a doubt after watching your entrance video."

She blushed. "Well...that one doesn't really count. It was a stationary camera shot. Not my best work."

"I disagree. It was an award-worthy short."

She giggled again, burying her head in his shoulder. Brie lay against him until the plane was ready to take off. She looked out of the window when the engines started. "I love this part. The roar of the engine, the shaking of the plane, and then that sick little feeling you get when you first lose contact with the ground." Brie sighed happily. "I love flying!"

"We'll see how much you love it ten hours from now."

She looked at him and smiled. "Sir, anywhere with you is lovely."

He shook his head, but she saw the slight upturn to his lips.

Once the plane was in the air, Sir put his seat all the way back. She followed his lead, turning towards him so she could stare at his handsome face.

"Don't just stare at me, Brie."

She looked away, embarrassed. "I can't help it, Sir."

He chuckled softly. "Make conversation then."

With permission given, Brie gazed at him again but

was silent for a moment. Her heart thumped in her chest as she built up courage to say the one thing that had been bothering her since their visit with her family.

"Sir, my parents seem to know more about your past than I do."

He looked at her with a somber expression. "Yes, it is unfair to you."

She didn't press further, but she waited expectantly.

He took a deep breath but then said nothing. Minutes passed in strained silence. Brie consoled herself that he still wasn't ready to talk about it. She was surprised when he finally spoke.

"You should know that my parents were envied when they were young. The two complemented each other like the sun complements the moon. He shone with brilliance; she equaled him in her loving reflection." He smiled, as if he was remembering something treasured.

But his smile faltered as he continued, "Unfortunately, my mother grew jealous of his fame, no longer content to act as his reflection. She found power in cheating on him behind his back. I became aware of her infidelity when I was thirteen, but I kept it hidden, thinking I was protecting him…" Sir paused. When he continued, his jaw was clenched as if it physically hurt him to speak the words.

"I remember the day as if it were yesterday. I can still smell the exhaust fumes from the school bus as it pulled up to my stop. I saw her car and *his*, and then my dad drove up in his Ferrari. He wasn't scheduled to arrive for another two days. I pushed my way through the line, trying to get off the bus, hoping I could prevent what was about to play out."

Sir closed his eyes, obviously reliving it in his mind. "I ran, but he had already disappeared into the house. I headed directly for the bedroom even though I knew it was too late. I entered the room to see my father pointing a gun at my mother. He vacillated between aiming it at her and the naked boy toy. For a second, I thought he would shoot her dead, but then he lowered it. The only thing he asked her was, 'Why?' My mother said nothing."

He opened his eyes and stared blankly ahead. "He turned to me and said, 'I'm sorry, son', put the gun to his head and pulled the trigger before I could move to stop him." Sir's voice caught, but he cleared his throat and continued. "I ran to him, begging him to hold on even though I knew…"

Sir turned to Brie, the rawness of his pain written clearly on his face. "I watched the life ebb from his eyes…heard his death rattle. It is a terrible thing to witness—the death of a loved one." Sir looked away. In the barest whisper he added, "It haunts me to this day."

Silent tears rolled down Brie's cheeks as she put her hand on Sir's and squeezed tightly, wanting to impart her strength.

His voice was devoid of emotion when he spoke again. "My mother was a convincing liar. She kept my father's estate and all his assets while she trashed his reputation to protect hers. She stripped everything from him… So I disowned her, legally distancing myself from the whore."

Brie braved a question. "How did you move on from

it, Sir?"

"I am my father's son. I must strive for excellence in everything I do. I went to college, graduated with honors. Even though I had sworn myself away from women, my Italian blood would not be satisfied. I was wired to explore the female body. Thankfully, Rytsar introduced me to the BDSM lifestyle in college. Although he has preferences that I do not share, I found the lifestyle itself fascinating. Yet, it was the level of trust required in the D/s relationship that was the most appealing. It was the only sane choice for me."

"I'm glad you found a way to move past it, Sir."

"On the outside it may appear that way, but for most of my adult life I have been emotionally dead. My satisfaction has been in helping others explore their limits, because I have been unwilling to explore mine."

"And now, Sir?"

In answer, he covered her in a blanket and put the mask over her eyes. "Try to sleep, Brie. I have a feeling Durov is going to keep us entertained from the moment we land."

Brie woke to Sir's light touch. "We're here."

She popped up in her seat and pulled off the mask, then quickly gathered her things. "I can't believe it!" she whispered, conscious of the other travelers still snoozing. She was thrilled to be one of the first ones off the plane. Sir led her to the immigration area, where she was confronted with the long lines.

"And this is where we wait," Sir said with resignation.

Brie pulled out her passport in anticipation, but the lines weren't moving. She craned her neck to see what the holdup was just as a severe-looking security guard with mirrored sunglasses grabbed the passport from her hand.

"Hey!"

Sir tried to take it back, but two similar men showed up. The one with her passport took Brie by the arm, dragging her away. Sir attempted to follow her, but the other two men held him back. He fought against them, but was unable to break free.

"Brie, I will come for you! Don't do anything or say anything until I find you."

"Sir!" she cried, reaching out for him.

She was led to a small room filled with black and white monitors. Once they were inside, the door was locked and she was directed to sit down by a daunting woman built like a bulldozer. Brie sat down reluctantly, noticing another male guard behind her. She had no idea what was happening and was tempted to make a break for the door.

The large woman snapped a command Brie did not understand. The woman said it again and tried to spread her legs apart.

Brie fought against her, slapping the woman's hands away. *Are they going to do a body cavity search?* She began to panic.

"*Nyet!*" Brie cried, saying one of three words she

knew in Russian.

The male guard behind her leaned in, inches from her face. All she could see was the reflection of her own terrified expression. He said in perfect English, "Open your legs."

I know that voice!

Brie timidly removed the sunglasses and looked into his piercing blue eyes. "Rytsar."

He stood up and rocked the room with his laughter. "*Radost moya*, you recognize your previous Master. I'm impressed."

Brie glanced at the screens and saw a camera shot of Sir. He was still fighting against the two guards. Rytsar followed her gaze. "Ah, yes. My friend is not happy, is he?"

He nodded to the woman, who immediately left. "I wanted to spare you both the long lines, but... Well, I could not help amusing myself. What do you expect from a sadist?"

A sadist?

She looked at the friendly Russian Dom again, be-lieving he was just making a joke. Brie turned her attention back to the screen and watched as Sir was taken out of the line.

Rytsar's mirth greeted Sir as he entered the small room. "All is well, *moy droog*. Your sub has not been touched."

Sir held out his arms and Brie raced to them, grateful to be in his protective embrace.

"She seems to be satisfied with you. Would not even open her legs for me," Rytsar said, chuckling.

Sir kissed the top of Brie's head. "I'd forgotten your propensity for practical jokes. Should have seen this one coming."

"Yes, I was surprised you did not. However, it was far more amusing that you didn't." He smiled charmingly at them both. "Shall we be off, then? I am anxious to introduce you to my friends."

Brie was surprised to learn that Rytsar lived in an old mansion. She should have suspected it with all the aristocrat talk, but she'd never quite believed it until they pulled up to the large estate. The impressive red brick home even sported narrow turrets, giving it a regal appearance.

"This is really your home?" she asked in awe.

"It has been in the Durov line for centuries," he replied without arrogance.

Brie glanced at Sir. He seemed unaffected by the grandeur. She decided to take his lead and not react to the splendor of the place, even as they walked through the halls and she saw the gold accents, painted ceilings, and antique furniture begging to be admired.

"Please take a moment to refresh yourselves before you join us in the dungeon. My friends are dying to meet my American comrade and his new sub."

All Brie heard was the word 'dungeon'.

"I assume we just head downwards?" Sir inquired.

"Titov will direct you." Rytsar pointed to a servant, who nodded curtly.

"Fine." Sir took Brie's hand and guided her upstairs. Once inside the privacy of the room, Sir gathered her into his arms. "I know this seems a bit much, but I did warn you. Rytsar has eccentric tastes. It's not too surprising he has his own dungeon."

Brie thought back to Rytsar's statement that he was a sadist. It conjured all kinds of frightening scenarios. "Will I be asked to scene, Sir?" she squeaked.

"No. Tonight we are guests and will simply observe. It is no different than visiting one of our clubs back home. I suspect his friends want to show off their various talents. However, you should be aware that Rytsar's tastes run on the sadistic side. I am sure his friends are of equal bent."

Brie sighed nervously. Although she had witnessed a few scenes at The Haven, it was not something she had personally sought out. Not having expressed interest in masochism, she had been spared the more sadistic side of BDSM play during her training.

"Take this opportunity to explore new horizons, Brie. It is part of the reason I chose to come here. It is my belief you cannot know your desires or limits unless you expose yourself to them."

Brie understood Sir's reasoning and even agreed with it, and yet she still felt uneasy about exploring the darker side of pain.

The Dungeon

The two followed Titov down a long flight of circular stairs. Before they reached the bottom, Brie heard screams echoing from the other side of the door. She swallowed hard and tried to keep a peaceful countenance.

Sir whispered in her ear, "Remember, the subs are masochists. This is their preference."

Brie nodded as they entered. The cries quickly died down as everyone turned to look at them.

Rytsar's voice rose over the crowd. "Welcome, *moy droog!*"

He walked over to greet them both. "We have been waiting impatiently for you." He turned to the crowd. "Please, continue the entertainment."

Immediately a whip cracked and a piercing scream filled the air.

Rytsar gestured proudly to the expansive underground room. "I have it all here. The ultimate playground of kink." Brie glanced around the dark and ominous dungeon. The floor was made of unforgiving stone, the walls of rough brick, and large wooden support beams dotted the room. Attached to the beams were chains and cuffs of various lengths and materials, some of which were already adorned with naked submissives.

In the farthest corner, Brie noticed several large metal cages. But the wall that held a plethora of whips, floggers, canes and other tools—the number of which was staggering—captivated her imagination and left her speechless.

The anguished cry of a submissive grabbed her attention. She glanced around at women bound to St. Andrew's crosses, benches, or leather swings, being whipped, fucked, or tortured with unknown instruments. Brie struggled to take it all in.

Sir felt her tension and suggested, "Why don't we visit the scenes individually, Durov? You can explain to my sub what is transpiring."

"Certainly," he said, nodding to Brie.

Rytsar guided them over to a woman spread out on a bench, bound by chains. She had a large metal collar around her neck, making it impossible for her to move. "Andreev enjoys subjecting his sub to clitoral torture." The Dom had already attached nipple clamps, but there was an extra chain that led down to her pussy. He was in the process of pulling back the hood of her clit and attaching the clamp to the loose skin. "Clit exposure allows for more intense play," Rytsar explained.

The Dom rubbed her naked clit, making the sub whimper pitifully. He then picked up a lit candle and leaned in, licking her erect clit before dripping the wax directly on the exposed sex. The girl screamed, but didn't call her safe word. Brie saw clearly that her pussy was red and swollen with excitement.

A more lustful cry caught Brie's attention. She turned to a lanky female chained to a pole being whipped with a cat o' nine tails. Rytsar grinned. "My personal favorite, the cat o' nines. Such exquisite torture."

She struggled to wrap her head around the fact Rytsar was a sadist. He had been demanding but playful the day she'd scened with him. Based on his actions that day, she never would have suspected his underlying need to deliver pain. Brie suddenly realized that what had been a mind-blowing experience for her must have been mere child's play for him.

As Rytsar continued to show off his dungeon, she kept glancing back at the girl on the pole. Despite her pained screams, the Dom had already made the girl come twice. Brie couldn't help wondering if she was missing out somehow. All of the women in this dungeon seemed to be thoroughly enjoying themselves despite—or because of—the pain.

Later that night, when she was lying in bed, safe in Sir's arms, she broached the subject. "Master, do you have sadistic tendencies?"

He did not answer her question; instead, he correctly read into her inquiry and turned it back on her. "Has tonight's exposure awakened a latent desire, téa?"

Clever Master.

"I was frightened by some of the things I saw to-night, but I wonder, Sir…is it a true fear or just fear of the unknown?"

"I noticed your interest in the cat o' nines," he commented, nibbling her neck. "Would you like to taste its sting?"

She hesitated, the idea of it unsettling—yet alluring. "Yes."

"Then I shall speak to Durov tomorrow."

"What? Aren't you going to scene with me?"

"No. I shall defer to Rytsar Durov's expertise."

"Then I would rather not," she answered quickly.

"I believe you should," he replied, sucking on her earlobe. "How else can you know your desires if you do not explore them?"

She tried to imagine herself tied to the pole receiving painful strokes, but as much as it enticed her, it frightened her equally as much. "Will you be there with me, Sir?"

"No, Brie. I would detract from the scene." She tensed in his arms. "Do not fret, little sub. I will request a simple whipping session, no audience and no intercourse involved."

She nestled deeper into his arms, suddenly excited and terrified by the prospect of scening with Rytsar. "What if I only last one stroke, Sir?"

"Then you will know where your limit lies. This is an exploration, not an endurance test."

She smiled and kissed him. "Yes, Sir."

She closed her eyes, reminding herself of that the next

day, when she was naked and bound in chains before Rytsar.

The broad-chested Russian removed his shirt and smiled down at her. "I am thrilled to introduce you to my 'nines', *radost moya.*" He held up his multi-tailed whip reverently so she could admire it. The baldheaded Dom walked around her slowly. She remembered the ferociousness of the dragon tattooed on his muscle-bound shoulder. Like the dragon, Rytsar was beautiful—but dangerous.

Goosebumps rose on her skin as he caressed her with the tails, her body anticipating the violent sensations the knots were about to provoke. He pressed the handle to her lips. "Hold it, while I prepare you."

Brie opened her mouth. The leather tasted of the salt from his hands. He proceeded to twist her hair, pulling her head back. The chains clanked in reaction to the sudden movement. "We shall see how deep your dark fantasies lie, my willing sub." He deftly tied her long hair into a knot with a leather string.

Rytsar had already placed a Magic Wand between her legs and bound her to it so that the vibrator was firmly pressed against her clit. Once her arms were pulled taut above her head, he turned the wicked toy on. She squirmed, her pussy instantly responding to the vibration.

"I use this tool on submissives new to the dungeon. It helps acclimate them to the ecstasy of pain."

She moaned, a quiet panic setting in. The dark oppression of the dungeon, along with the lonely silence of the great room, made her anxious. However, it was the nagging sense of fear that had her entire body on alert.

Rytsar ran his hands over her naked skin. "I can feel your fear, *radost moya*. It...turns me on."

It was disconcerting to think her genuine fear was an aphrodisiac for the Russian Dom.

"Subjecting a submissive to intense pain is much like deflowering a virgin. I enjoy the journey of penetrating a sub's will with my desire."

Brie realized she was breathing erratically and forced herself to calm down, afraid of fainting before they even began. Rytsar walked away from her and towards the wall of instruments. With growing dread, she watched as he thoughtfully chose a malicious-looking flogger from the wall.

Rytsar did not explain himself. He simply walked back to her, cutting the air with the whip to warm up his muscles.

Brie closed her eyes, readying herself for the initial stroke, but *nothing* could prepare her for the fire he evoked. She salivated against the tangy leather of his cat o' nines, trying to keep her cries at bay as Rytsar lashed her back with solid, unyielding strokes. She whimpered loudly, the chains dancing around her as she rocked against the force of his blows. This was no gentle warm-up.

The sound of her lashing echoed throughout the dungeon, filling her ears. She did not drop the handle from her mouth to call out her safe word, but tears ran down her face as she forced herself to accept the on-slaught.

When Rytsar finally stopped, the air seemed to still

reverberate with the echoes of her surrender. He came up behind her, caressing her cheek. "The tenseness of your muscles, the whimpers against the leather, your sweet, sweet tears…they call to me." He caressed her fiery back and then patted her ass lightly before giving the Wand a small adjustment. Brie moaned as she focused on the intense vibration, which helped to cut through the wall of pain.

"Your body must grow used to my pleasure. Much like a child learning to walk, it requires guidance." His hot breath caressed her ear as he whispered, "You're quite desirable right now, *radost moya*. So vulnerable and scared. It takes strength not to ravish you."

He laid the flogger down and took the cat o' nines from her lips. He slowly wiped her saliva from his instrument, dragging out the anticipation. "This will hurt. I make no excuses. I want it to hurt. I want you to react to the pain." He abruptly threw the towel down and moved into position behind her.

This scene was unlike any experience she'd ever had. He wasn't trying to 'carry' her into subspace; he was taking her there kicking and screaming. *I want this*, she reminded herself as fresh tears ran down her cheeks. Brie was determined to face this fear, to embrace the experience despite the fact she was terrified.

"Focus on your clit as I strip your back," he commanded, just before the first lash of the tails came into contact with her skin. All illusions of bravery evaporated as she released an all-out scream. There was no controlling this pain. It was sharp, cruel, and more terrible than she'd ever imagined.

A second stroke immediately followed, not allowing her even a breath between. She shrieked, pulling against the chains, her back feeling as if it had been laid open and raw.

Then she felt his hot breath against her cheek. "Color?"

Brie gasped, "Red...ish yellow." There was a part of Brie that desired to know if she could defeat the pain, overcome its fierce power and enter subspace.

"Good," he replied. He reached between her legs and turned up the vibrator.

Brie threw her head back, her whole body shaking. Maybe the next hit would be enlightening or stimulating on a level she hadn't experienced before. *Fear will not control me!*

She heard each step magnified as he repositioned himself. She felt the swing of the cat o' nines before it came anywhere close to her. Her scream erupted when the evil knots impacted on her skin. Hot lava radiated from each point the cat o' nines made contact with her back. Rytsar followed it up with a second, equally forceful stroke.

Brie screamed and then sobbed uncontrollably. This was not pleasurable or enlightening. It simply hurt beyond anything she had ever experienced—and she couldn't handle it any longer. "No more," she begged between sobs, "no more..."

"So soon, *radost moya*?" Rytsar stroked the back of her neck lightly several times and then grasped it possessively, making her knees weak. She swayed back and forth in the chains, while the vibrator between her legs continued its relentless teasing.

"I have so much more I wish you to experience."

There was an urging in her spirit to acquiesce to his need, but her lessons at the Submissive Training Center had prepared her for moments such as this. She shook her head and called out clearly, "Red."

He chuckled. She felt his sharp teeth as he bit the back of her neck, wrapping his arm around her tightly. A deep and startling orgasm shook through her body. Brie twitched in her bonds until it had passed, completely stunned by it.

Rytsar kissed the bite marks he'd left before releasing her from the chains and removing the toy from between her legs. He had to support her as she stumbled to a padded table nearby. The Dom directed her to lie on her stomach.

She jumped when she first felt the icy salve. Rytsar smoothed it onto her wounds as he spoke in a low, calming voice. He shared his memories of their first encounter, recalling details that brought the scene back to life.

"My American captive…beautiful, passionate, frightened but willing. It is a good memory for me."

She smiled, nodding her agreement. Brie vividly recalled that day. She'd been inexperienced when he'd won her at the auction, yet he had managed to fulfill her fantasy in every sense of the word while making her feel worthy of his attentions.

As Rytsar continued to reminisce, his masculine hands gently tended to the wounds he had inflicted. His aftercare was so tender, so kind; it almost made up for the pain she'd endured under his hands.

When he had finished, Rytsar helped her off the table and gathered her into his arms, albeit carefully. "You did well, *radost moya*. Your Master will be pleased."

She shook her head against his chest, not buying it.

He murmured seductively, "I can help you learn to enjoy the pain."

She had no doubt he had the ability, but it was not what she desired. Brie worried Sir would be disappointed as she walked behind Rytsar back to her Master.

Sir immediately put down his work and stood up when they entered the room. "How was the experience?" he asked Brie.

Her bottom lip trembled in answer.

He turned to Rytsar with a look of concern. "How did she fare, Durov?"

"It was a decent beginning."

Sir looked her over again, his eyes unreadable.

Rytsar kissed the back of Brie's hand before returning her to Sir's care. She dropped to the floor and bowed stiffly before the Russian Dom. "Thank you, Rytsar Durov."

He nodded his acknowledgement and slapped Sir on the shoulder. "Trainable, but no masochist."

"I suspected as much," Sir replied evenly.

Rytsar bade them goodbye and left them to their own devices.

Sir helped Brie off the floor and smoothed her worried brow with his fingers. "That is fortunate news, téa, for I am no sadist."

Performance

Rytsar spent the daylight hours while they were there taking the two all over Moscow, introducing them to the cuisine, the culture, and national treasures like St. Basil's Cathedral in Red Square, and the quiet grandeur of the Novodevichy Cemetery. Brie was amazed by the history represented all around her and the many riches to be found in the numerous museums. However, it was the smiles of the Russian people she treasured most. She had expected stoic faces greeting her on the crowded streets, but she was met by grins and snatches of English wherever she went.

Sir had specifically instructed her to act vanilla outside the confines of Rytsar's home. "I want you to interact with the culture. It will serve you well in your career. Experience the nuances of every culture you encounter."

That freedom allowed Brie to fully drink in the foreign environment. She smelled, touched and tasted everything she could, and interacted with anyone who gave her a sideways glance.

When they weren't sightseeing, they were enjoying the unique entertainment provided by their host. Rytsar spared no expense showing his good friends all that Russia had to offer, including a private performance of a well-known Russian opera. However, there was a condition to admission to this particular performance.

As Sir zipped up her sleek, crystal-studded gown, he casually mentioned to Brie, "Durov has asked you and me to entertain his guests this evening."

She waited until he'd finished to turn around and ask him, "I thought we were going to an opera, Sir?"

"We are. Our performance takes place after the show."

Her heart skipped a beat. "What kind of performance?"

He turned her back towards the mirror, looking at her in the reflection. "Durov has asked us to scene together. He wishes his comrades to observe a different type of power play. Durov was greatly influenced by what he observed visiting America as a college student."

Sir had insisted she wear her hair up for the evening, giving him free access to her neck. He kissed the nape of it tenderly. "It changed the flavor of Durov's sadism, so to speak."

"May I ask how, Sir?"

Sir looked at her thoughtfully. "Suffice to say, his partner's satisfaction is of consequence to him now. It was not always the case."

Brie lowered her gaze, a shudder going through her. She had watched Rytsar scene several times since her session with him. He was hard on his submissives, sometimes frighteningly so, but he knew how to please them and he was affectionate afterwards. What he had been like before, she could only imagine.

It made her think, though… All of Rytsar's friends were sadists. The submissives they played with were experienced masochists.

"Is something wrong?" Sir asked.

She forced herself to reply, even though she was reluctant to voice her inadequacy to him. "Sir, I am but a child compared to the submissives these men are used to."

"Do you put down my sub so easily, téa?"

Brie bowed her head, smiling to herself. How easy Sir made it to be his. "No, Master."

"Tonight we will play out a short scene of my choosing. Nothing elaborate. Just a Master playing with his sub for the pleasure of others."

She nodded, still looking at the floor.

"Téa."

She looked up, gazing into his warm, confident eyes as he turned her back around. "All that is required is that you please me. No one else in the room matters."

Brie breathed in his truth. *No one else matters…*

Sir escorted her down to the front row of the mini-theatre in Rytsar's mansion, so that all the men in attendance could admire her. Brie's nipples instantly became erect in response to their intense stares. Everyone knew they were the entertainment for the evening—after the opera.

Brie sat down with practiced poise in between Rytsar and Sir. The Russian nodded to her pleasantly, but said nothing. He lifted his finger and the lights dimmed just before the curtains opened.

Sir leaned towards her and whispered, "This is the Russian opera *Ruslan and Lyudmila*. It's one of the few Russian operas that are more...fanciful in nature." He kissed her cheek. "I think you will enjoy it, téa."

He was acting as if they were simply there to enjoy the performance, so she followed his example and focused solely on the opera. Brie was enthralled by the lavish costumes and extravagant sets that graced the stage. The actors must have been true performers because their voices were exceptional, ringing strong and true. The same could be said of the talented musicians. Rytsar had not provided a simple home performance; this was on par with any Broadway show.

Brie held her breath when the flying dragon appeared on the stage. The huge creature was made of billowing bolts of gold silk. It was enchanting and otherworldly. But she was horrified when the opera took a brutal turn, making her question Sir's assurance she would enjoy it. It wasn't until the final act that all was made right. The ending was wonderful and sweet, the way only fairytales can be.

Brie clapped her hands zealously when the curtains finally closed.

"I see that you enjoyed yourself," Rytsar commented

with satisfaction.

"Very much, Rytsar Durov. It was…magnificent."

"I would have to agree," Sir interjected. "You sur-
passed my expectations."

"Not an easy thing to do, peasant," the Russian replied, laughing. "But I was determined."

"It's an experience I will never forget," Brie ex-
claimed. "Never!"

"I hope to say the same of your performance."

Brie suddenly felt lightheaded. She was about to scene in front of the prominent Doms of Moscow.

"Without the expensive costumes and sets, all eyes
will be on you," Rytsar continued. "Not exactly fair, is
it?"

"None of it is necessary," Sir replied matter-of-factly.
"In fact, I would go as far as to say it is not the action
itself, but the intention behind it, that truly carries a
scene."

Sir tilted Brie's chin up with his finger, giving her a
lingering look that said clearly, *I lead, you follow.* She
nodded in understanding and then proceeded to melt
when his firm lips met hers. She stood up with renewed
confidence when Sir offered his hand.

Rytsar led them out of the theater and across the
hall. Servants on either side of two massive wooden
doors opened them as the group approached. Brie
swallowed nervously as she passed through the doorway
into the unusual room. The floor was made of dark
wood a shade just shy of midnight and glossed to a
perfect sheen. A long, red carpet made a path to a small,
low-lying table made of gold in the center of the large

room.

The table itself was encircled by unlit candles lining the floor. As she walked towards it, she noted the single line of chairs had been set six feet back, surrounding the table in a horseshoe pattern. The unusual seating allowed not only for the unobstructed view of the table, but also of a huge mirror on the opposite wall.

Brie began trembling as Sir guided her to the table. She had to step over the barrier of candles that separated them from the audience. Sir placed his hands on her shoulders, turning her towards the mirror. "Look at me, téa." She looked into the reflection as the men gathered and sat down. She understood now—the mirror was there to enhance the experience for both the participants and the observers.

He whispered in her ear, "Focus on your Master."

As she looked at Sir in the mirror, her confidence returned. When all of the gentlemen were seated, the doors closed and Brie heard the distinct sound of a large metal bar sliding into place. It added a thrill of fear, knowing they were locked in. For better or worse, she was to remain until the scene was complete. Thankfully, she was in Sir's trusted hands.

Rytsar spoke to the group in Russian. After his speech, he repeated it in English for their benefit. "We have come tonight to enjoy the unique performance of Sir Davis and his submissive, téa. They have witnessed our brand of dominance and have consented to share a scene of their own. Sit back and enjoy their unique dynamic."

Rytsar nodded to Sir before he sat down. The circle

of Doms was so near that she could hear their subtle movements and even smell their various colognes. It was unsettling to have the audience so close. Brie looked into the mirror again. *Sir...*

She watched as he slowly unzipped her gown. Then he kissed her neck as he eased the material off her shoulders. The dress fell and pooled at her feet. Suddenly she was naked except for her garters, fishnet stockings and six-inch heels. Exactly the way Sir preferred her.

His hands roved over her breasts, and then he began pinching and squeezing her nipples as he lowered his lips onto her bare shoulder. His eyes did not leave her as he looked at her reflection. She was mesmerized by his hungry gaze.

Brie tilted her chin upwards and pressed the back of her head against his chest, giving in to the magic of his caress. She tapped into the sexual energy of those around her and ground her body against her Master.

He lifted her right arm above her head and ran his fingers down the side of her breast, the concave of her waist and the swell of her hips, tickling her skin with his light caress. Then he turned to a servant, who handed him a long red cord. Sir doubled up the rope and then began to tie it around her right forearm, starting at the wrist, creating an intricate, braided pattern as he went.

She watched, fascinated by the Kinbaku feel of it. He tied the cord off at her elbow, leaving the ends to hang like a fringe. He leaned in and said, for her ears only, "A warrior's cuff."

Her interest was piqued as he raised her arm again. The vibrant shade of red radiated power and his words infused her with a sense of courage and purpose. She smiled at Sir in the reflection, suddenly feeling worthy of this public display.

One of her Master's hands glided over her stomach, then moved between her thighs, while the other captured her breast. She gasped as his fingers slid into her moist depths. She glanced at the mirror again. It was a visual representation of their relationship. He the masterful, confident Dominant and she the powerful, yet wholly devoted sub.

"Lie facedown on the table, arms and legs out-stretched," he commanded quietly.

Brie slid onto the table with catlike grace and laid herself out for him. Sir took his time as he removed her shoes, stockings and garters. His movements were sensual and confident, making her wet with anticipation.

She was startled to hear the sound of chains as Sir pulled up a cuff from underneath the table. It was attached to the leg. He secured her wrist, glancing at her briefly with a smirk. He continued until she was completely chained to the table.

So far he had done nothing more than undress her and bind her, but she was already quivering with need. It would not take much to set her body humming.

Sir nodded and a servant handed him a large swab and container. Brie glanced to the right and saw another servant standing with an extinguisher held elegantly in his hands. *So it's to be fire play tonight.* No wonder Sir had insisted she put her hair up.

The servant lit the swab and stepped back just before the lights lowered. The room was completely silent.

There was no accompanying music for the scene. Brie found it made for a more intimate connection with the audience. Every movement of Sir's, every gasp from her lips was heard by their observers.

And Brie did gasp when she felt the cool alcohol coat her skin. Sir began with her back, making simple designs, lighting them on fire before he swept them out with his hand. He moved down her legs and even lit the soles of her feet, making her yelp when heat from the flames licked the sensitive areas.

As with the undressing, Sir took his time, building anticipation for both Brie and the audience. She noticed that Sir let the flames burn longer as he advanced in the scene. It required more of her concentration, as the heat was intense. Each time she was just about to cry out 'yellow', Sir would wipe the flames from her skin.

He began creating more detailed patterns on her back. Brie wondered if the designs had significance, because the men grunted in response when he lit them on fire.

Then he spoke the first words since he'd asked her to lie on the table. "You and I seek the path together." She felt him making a trail of a spiral circle with the cool liquid. Brie held her breath as he tapped it with the flame. The fire danced down the path he'd created.

He swiped it away and made a new design. She could identify the sideways eight easily, knowing exactly what the symbol meant. "No matter what the future brings, you and I are connected."

Sir lit the symbol for infinity on her back. She let it burn not only on her skin, but into her soul, almost regretful when he swept it away.

He then lit the ring of candles on the floor, one by one, before putting out the fire in his hand.

Brie looked into the mirror and felt a pleasant chill when she realized Sir was staring at her, his look cavernous in its depth and intensity. She could fall into those eyes, losing herself forever…

With the same slow precision he'd used to tie her up, Sir undid her bindings. He pulled her towards him on the smooth surface of the table and ordered her onto her hands and knees. He took off his clothes, his gaze never leaving hers in the reflection of the mirror. He caressed her bare mound gently and then smacked her on the ass. The satisfying sound of it echoed in the room and low chuckles emerged from the men.

He explored her pussy again, concentrating his efforts on her clit. "No coming," he instructed, rubbing at just the right tempo to start the chain reaction. Brie bit her lower lip when Sir slid his fingers into her pussy, going straight for her G-spot. She gasped when he caressed it, rolling his finger over the area slowly, pleasurably, until her body pulsed with electricity. He pulled his finger out and replaced it with his shaft.

Brie moaned when she felt his cock press against her. He smiled in the mirror, shaking his head in response to her unspoken request. Sir thrust forcefully, filling her with one solid stroke.

She arched her back to take the full length of him, holding back tears of joy as her Master claimed her. Brie watched as he grabbed her hips and began fucking her without restraint. It was an erotic scene, with the red warrior cuff he'd made contrasting against her white skin, the curves of her round ass in his hands, and the look of ecstasy on her Master's face.

Brie let out a primal scream that echoed throughout the room, desperate to express her passion and need for Sir. He met it with a roar of his own as he emptied his essence deep inside her.

He pulled her up to him, one arm across her chest, the other hand concentrated on her pussy. "Come for me, téa," he whispered through gritted teeth.

Brie threw her head back and allowed all the emotion and sexual electricity to release at once. She writhed in his arms as the powerful climax washed over her, blurring her senses. Afterwards, she lay against him like a ragdoll.

Sir murmured in her ear, "My beautiful goddess, see how you have captivated the audience."

Brie glanced discreetly at the men surrounding them. Their eyes were trained on her, holding varying looks of admiration and ravenous need. It was empowering to be admired by so many Doms, but she knew the truth.

"Master," she whispered.

"Yes, téa?"

"No one else in the room matters but you."

The Taking

Katia, one of Rytsar's favorite submissives, insisted on taking Brie out for a day of shopping. With only a few more days left before her return to the States, the Russian beauty with grey-green eyes suggested taking Brie to bargain for souvenirs at the Izmaylovo Market, a place popular for its rows upon rows of folk art, jewelry, and Russian crafts.

Sir gave his blessing, but told Brie before she left, "I have arranged a special rendezvous for us today. Do not get so caught up in your shopping that you resist."

"Of course not, Sir."

"Do not resist," he repeated. She noticed the glint in his eye, hinting of something clandestine. She felt a tingling in her loins. *Is there a kidnapping in my future?*

Brie spent hours perusing the individual shops, constantly on the lookout for Sir, but he didn't show. Eventually she stopped anticipating his arrival and immersed herself in the joys of bargaining with the shopkeepers and joking around with Katia.

After an especially good bargaining session, Katia

suggested they celebrate. "Shall we stop for a drink, Bennett-téa?"

Brie liked the cute nickname Katia had given her, combining her last name with Sir's pet name. With her hands already full of purchases, she readily agreed. "Sounds lovely!"

Brie tried to keep up with her long-legged friend as they navigated the backstreets of the city, but it was a struggle with her bulky packages. "Wait, Katia!" she shouted when the girl rounded a corner ahead of her. Brie ran to catch up, but couldn't find her when she made it to the corner. She ran on to the next street, but couldn't find Katia anywhere. Brie doubled back, not knowing what else to do.

Chills went down her spine when she first heard the confident footsteps behind her. Even though she knew it must be Sir, her survival instincts kicked in. The feeling of being chased was frightening even though it was thrilling, causing a reaction she had no control over. Brie understood she wasn't supposed to show resistance, but she got ready to bolt.

A strong hand covered her mouth, pulling her roughly backwards. Brie's cries were muffled as she fought for her freedom. She was dragged, kicking and screaming, into a van and then everything went dark as the door slammed shut.

"Shhhh…shhhh…" her captor whispered as his powerful arms held her tight against him. Brie realized she was in the hands of Rytsar and whimpered, relieved but still suffering from the adrenaline rush of her abduction.

He forcibly bound her wrists and ankles together, securing them so that she was properly hogtied and unable to move. Before he placed the gag over her mouth he kissed her deeply, his tongue caressing the inside of her mouth.

Brie heard another man speak Russian. He was out of her line of sight, but she could have sworn it was her Master. The men's exchange was lively. If it was indeed Sir, she suspected he was giving Rytsar a hard time for kissing her. The van screeched to a halt and the two switched places, with Rytsar now at the wheel.

She was rolled onto her side and blindfolded. Hands roved over her body, rough and demanding, but she knew with certainty it was Sir. He ripped at her clothes, exposing both her breasts and pussy. Then he pressed his hand against her bare mound and spoke Russian in a low, ominous tone as he pushed his fingers inside her. Instantly, she became a willing but helpless captive.

Brie moaned into the gag when his lips landed on her skin and she felt his teeth on her neck. Sir knew exactly how to subdue her for play. She did not move or make a sound as he rolled her onto her stomach.

Brie wondered if this was a take on her warrior fantasy. She quivered at the thought of her pleasure being increased twofold. There seemed to be only one problem—it didn't appear Sir wanted to share her.

Brie giggled into her gag.

Sir fisted her hair, pulling her head back. He growled into her ear, sending shivers of fearful pleasure as he ripped away the remainder of her skirt and slapped her ass hard. He let go of her then and moved away. It was her punishment for getting out of character.

That will not happen again, Master, she promised him silently.

Brie wondered where they were taking her and what their plans were. She knew they weren't going back to the mansion, because the drive had been far too long already. She'd lain on her stomach for so long that she was desperate to catch a full breath. Brie wiggled slightly in an attempt to find a more comfortable position, but was unsuccessful and groaned in distress. Sir quickly turned her on her side, brushing his hand over her body before abandoning her again.

Rytsar said something and the two started arguing. Brie wondered if Rytsar had wanted her to suffer for longer, but he did not have the final say—which seemed to irk the Dom. It was certainly interesting having best friends scene together like this.

Brie was extremely grateful to Sir for rolling her over. Even though Rytsar's hogtie was exciting in its tightness and constraint, she found it far more provocative now that she could breathe again. It gave her the opportunity to fantasize about what was going to happen. Brie couldn't stop herself from imagining taking both Sir and Rytsar at the same time, but she immediately dismissed the idea. Sir had been much too quick to switch places with Rytsar after the Russian had kissed her. It appeared that her Master was a possessive lover... Brie thought back on her warrior fantasy. It revolved around a young maiden losing her virginity. She was curious what 'virginal' territories these two planned to plunder.

The van slowed to a stop and she heard Rytsar exit

the vehicle. The door of the van slid open and the
northern wind blasted in, taking her breath away. Brie
was dragged to the cold edge of the van's floor and
covered in a blanket before she was lifted up and carried
between both men.

They spoke in hushed tones, possibly going over the
sequence of events. The men stopped, and then she
heard a key in a lock and the creak of a door being
swung open. The instant they walked over the threshold,
the warmth and crackling sounds of a fire greeted her.
She was carried to another room and thrown unceremo-
niously on a hard bed.

The blanket was ripped away. She felt the hands of
both men pulling off the remnants of her clothes—the
squeezing of a breast, the rubbing of her wet clit—and
then they were gone.

She listened to them moving about, the clinking of
glasses and laughter. Were they celebrating her capture
or what was about to commence? Her loins contracted in
pleasure at the thought of two highly experienced Doms
playing with her.

Brie heard someone enter the room. She whimpered,
keeping to her character but also hoping to instigate a
response. The low rumble that escaped from his lips let
her know it was Rytsar. She stiffened as he approached,
unsure of his intent, remembering their last session
together quite clearly.

His hands were rough as he untied her from her
bonds and removed the gag and blindfold. Then he
massaged her limbs, loosening up the muscles that had
been bound for so long. But the handsome Dom was

not finished. He proceeded to bind her wrists together again. Then his hand trailed down her body until he grasped her ankle and secured it to a leg of the simple bed set in the center of the room. He did the same with the other.

"Please don't hurt me," she begged, keeping in character but secretly meaning it. He grunted in reply, his face remaining stoic—not a reassuring response. Rytsar grabbed her bound wrists and pulled her towards him so that her body was completely stretched and her head hung over the edge of the bed. He secured her wrists so that she was immobile.

Despite her real fear, Brie's pussy responded to his rough treatment, moistening itself for possible entry.

He chuckled to himself as he looked her over, obviously pleased with his work. He called out to Sir, who entered with a smile on his face. Sir's expression quickly changed to one of lustful avarice when he beheld his helpless sub.

He nodded to Rytsar and then gazed back at her. The intensity of his stare made her squirm. She was no longer his submissive—she was his powerless captive.

Sir descended on her, surprising her with the fierceness of his kiss. He grabbed her long curls in one hand and her chin in the other, forcing his tongue deep into her mouth. At the same time, she felt Rytsar's fingers on her inner thigh. He said something wicked-sounding in Russian as he explored the folds of her wet pussy. She groaned as the Dom expertly teased her clit.

Sir's kiss suddenly became more heated. He released her face and his hands moved down to her breasts. He flicked her nipples, making them taut before his lips left hers and he encased one with his eager mouth. He sucked hard on one while continuing to pull and tease the other.

Meanwhile, Rytsar rimmed the entrance of her pussy with his fingers without penetrating. Brie's body instinctively tried to arch in response, but could not because of the restrictive bindings. It caused a gush of moistness that Rytsar rubbed against her already sensitive clit, causing her pussy to contract in delicious pleasure. As soon as he felt her respond, Rytsar pulled away and left the bed.

Brie concentrated on Sir. He'd pressed her breasts together and was sucking each nipple alternately. She thrust her head back, giving in to the electrical current he was shooting directly to her groin.

Then she heard it…the distinctive sound of the Magic Wand. This time Brie's whimper was quite real. Rytsar chuckled under his breath, anticipating the orgasmic torture he was about to unleash. Brie's whole body tensed when she felt the vibration on her pussy.

Sir pinched her nipples as his lips returned to her mouth. She closed her eyes as her whole body began to tremble with the vibration. The Russian Dom was forcing a quick orgasm. However, Rytsar commanded, "*Nyet*," just as she was about to crest.

Brie cried out as she fought against the desperate need to release. Sir pinched her nipples harder, giving her something to latch onto other than the fire within her loins. With a valiant effort, she avoided the orgasm.

Rytsar seemed pleased and eased up on the vibrating

pressure against her clit. Sir got up and moved to the head of the bed. He unzipped his pants and presented her with a raging hard-on.

Brie looked up at him, but did not open her mouth, in keeping with her character. He pressed his cock against her lips. The warmth of it enticed her. She pretended reluctance as she opened her mouth and he forced the head of his shaft inside.

"*Sosat' moy chlen*," he commanded gruffly.

There was no need to translate that order. Brie began sucking his cock with timid relish. While Sir enjoyed her services, Rytsar pressed the vibrator against her clit with renewed fervor.

Brie moaned on Sir's cock as Rytsar played with her pussy. She took it all in, loving the dual attention. Her mouth was delightfully occupied by her Master while her clit danced with the vibrator.

Master thrust deeper down her throat, demanding full access. She relaxed her muscles to allow his sexy invasion. However, Rytsar was not playing fair and she found herself about to come again without any warning.

"*Nyet,*" the Russian Dom said with amusement.

Brie's muffled cries met his command.

Sir stroked her throat with his hands, feeling the swell of his cock inside her. The pressure of his fingers distracted her enough to stave off the climax, but just barely.

Rytsar eased the vibration momentarily. Brie wasn't sure how much she could take, but all her concerns fell away when Sir held onto her face with both hands and began fucking her mouth. Suddenly, it was just the two of them as he derived pleasure from her throat and she reveled in giving her body over to him. Brie closed her eyes and drifted into an ethereal bliss.

Instead of coming in her throat, Sir pulled out and released on her chest. She moaned with satisfaction as he spread his semen over her skin. It was a psychological and visual claiming. "I am Sir's..." she murmured aloud.

Rytsar's blue eyes flashed with impish joy as he pressed the vibrator against her and turned it onto the higher setting. She had no hope and whimpered in protest.

Sir knelt down by her head and growled passionately into her ear. She felt a deep contraction in her pussy in response to his voice. Then she heard the welcome word, *"Da,"* come from her Master's lips. She followed his order and came fiercely in honor of both men. Her hips could not lift into the air, so she remained still as the muscles of her vagina pulsed powerfully and her feminine juices flowed in release.

The wand was removed and then Brie felt Rytsar's warm tongue as he gave her still reverberating sex a prolonged lick, while Sir seized her mouth and kissed her deeply. The double kiss was the perfect ending to the scene, and Brie sighed in satisfaction when they pulled away.

Rytsar began untying her ankles while Sir took care of her wrists. Her Master kissed her one more time before helping her to her feet. She wobbled a bit, weak from the session, so Master picked her up and slung her over his shoulder, carrying her through the spacious cabin to a bathroom in the back.

The place had a rustic feel, but everything was of the finest quality, including the tub. It was free-standing with golden claw-feet. He set her down and gently pushed her towards it. Obviously she was meant to clean up before the next scene. Brie immediately started the water as she watched Sir leave. She could barely hear their manly voices over the rushing water of the tap. It was deliciously provocative to contemplate what they might do next.

When she'd finished her bath, she was surprised to find Rytsar waiting for her just outside the doorway. He took hold of the back of her neck, sending a chill of possession through her. He guided her to the main room where Sir was waiting for them.

Her Master watched silently as Rytsar tied her to a chair. After binding her wrists behind her and her legs to the chair, he picked up a set of gold nipple clamps connected by a chain. He smiled as he manipulated each nipple, readying it for the clamp. Then he pulled on the sensitive skin, attaching the clamp to the areola so that when he released it, her nipple stood erect and begging for attention. Rytsar moved to the other, performing the same procedure before tightening the pressure on both.

The Russian Dom flicked her nipples playfully, sending an immediate burst of fire to her nether regions. She tilted her head back and closed her eyes, taking in the sensation. He made one quick swipe against her slit and grunted his approval before returning to Sir.

The two sat down at a small table and began a game of chess. With her nipples throbbing and her pussy wet, she watched the Doms battle it out in a contest of strategy and wit. They laughed and chatted in Russian the entire time, but there was an underlying intensity to their play. Despite being friends, the two were fierce competitors.

Watching the men play chess, she better understood their success as Doms. Each was able to see several moves ahead and anticipate what the other was planning. The two were closely matched, making it a long and passionate game.

Sir glanced at her several times during the match, apparently liking what he saw. Each time she felt his eyes on her, she melted inside. It would take only a simple touch and she would come for him. It was during one of his glances that Rytsar moved a piece without Sir's knowledge. When Master looked back at the board, Rytsar moved another piece and knocked Sir's king over with a smug smile.

Sir shook his head and looked over the board as if he couldn't believe it. Rytsar glanced at Brie and winked. It was a wicked thing to do. She debated whether to tell Sir, but found there was no need as he quickly identified the false move. He shot Rytsar a humorous look before knocking his king over and declaring himself the winner.

The two broke out in laughter. Then Sir looked at Brie again, his luminous eyes sucking her in, hypnotizing her. He stood up and she held her breath. As he approached, she squirmed in the chair, knowing the power of his touch. She whimpered when his lips came dangerously close to hers, and then he moved to her ear and whispered, "Téa."

Her pussy erupted in a small orgasm. Sir reached between her legs and felt the last of its tremors. He smiled before walking away, leaving her alone in the room with the Russian. She glanced in Rytsar's direction. He stared at her as if he held some dark and delectable secret he was unwilling to share.

Sir returned, dressed in a thick coat, boots and a traditional Russian hat. Brie had to admit he looked charming as a Russian and smiled bashfully at him when he approached. He was carrying a fur for her.

He put it down to release Brie from the chair. Before he untied her, he freed one nipple from the metal clamp, sucking hard on her breast to reduce the pain. She held her breath as he freed the other and encased her nipple with his warm suction. Brie groaned in pleasure. Sir looked up at her before releasing her nipple from his mouth with a sensual pop.

He undid the bindings, picked up the fur, then helped his naked sub into it. Her Master placed a matching hat on her head last, pulling it down over her ears. He gazed at her tenderly. "*Krasivaya.*"

She wasn't sure of the meaning, but knew by his tone that it was meant as a compliment. Brie wrapped her arms around his bulky frame and pressed against him. Sir helped her into her boots and then took her hand to lead her outside.

The scenery was unbelievably beautiful in its winter splendor. The cabin was next to a secluded lake covered in a thick sheet of ice. Large flakes drifted down lazily, changing direction only when a frigid breeze caught hold of them. She stuck out her tongue to catch one of the huge flakes and giggled when one landed on her nose and melted.

Instead of taking her to the lake, Sir headed into the forest. They walked until he stopped in front of an incredibly tall, ancient-looking tree. Sir pushed her back against it, and opened her coat without warning. The freezing air caressed her naked skin, making her nipples stand to attention, but soon Sir's warm hands were caressing them.

His fingers moved to her clit and he growled in English, "Your pussy has come twice, but it has not been satisfied. Let me remedy that." Sir unbuttoned his coat and fumbled with his pants. He pressed her against the tree as he thrust his cock inside her.

Brie cried out in satisfaction, overcome by the feeling of Master's shaft. So hard, so perfect, so needed… He grunted and lifted her up, giving her all of him. Her fur coat protected her from the roughness of the bark as he pushed into her with abandon.

"Oh, Sir! Oh, God, Sir, yes!" she cried.

He slowed down and looked into her eyes. "I love everything about you, Brie. Your passion, your mind, your body, your need…all of it." His lips landed on hers again as he made love to her in the forest. Brie watched the large flakes gather on his head and shoulders as he took her. It was magical, this unexpected coupling in the forest.

"I love you," she lifted her mouth to his ear, "Thane."

He went wild then, seeking deeper access. Her screams echoed in the forest as she gave herself over completely to his passion. His grunts soon turned into groans as he came close to climaxing.

She closed her eyes so she could feel the moment it happened—the thickening of his cock, the deeper thrusts as he released his essence. "Thank you, Sir. Thank you, Master," she murmured into his neck as he gave his final thrusts.

Sir pulled out and set her down, then buttoned up her coat and readjusted her hat. He whispered hoarsely, "I have one last surprise." He zipped his pants and buttoned his coat before taking her hand.

Master took her on a leisurely stroll back to the cabin, allowing her a chance to admire the winter scenery. He pointed out a herd of deer on the other side of the lake. Brie smiled, overcome by the natural beauty of the place. The mountains surrounding them were covered by clouds and the deep silence of the falling snow made it feel like they were the only people in the world.

Brie squeezed Sir's arm. "I love this place."

He patted her hand. "As do I, téa, as do I."

A Gift

When they returned to the cabin, Sir helped her out of her winter clothing and told her to warm herself by the fire. She gladly complied, curling up on the hearth as close to the warmth as her naked skin would allow.

Sir asked Rytsar in a joking tone, "Did you miss us?"

"You, no. *Radost moya*, yes."

He chuckled good-naturedly. "Fair enough. I find her company far more agreeable than yours as well."

Rytsar slapped him hard on the back. "Time for some vodka!" He marched to the kitchen and brought back three glasses and a plate of small pickles. He smiled gleefully at Brie. "Tonight we make you a real woman!"

Brie had avoided joining the drinking games the men had enjoyed nearly every night. Today it didn't look like that was going to be allowed. Rytsar handed her the first glass and passed the other one to Sir.

"Brie, you are expected to drink it in one gulp," Sir reminded her.

She looked at the large amount Rytsar had poured

into the glass and shook her head.

"Do not insult the host," Rytsar reprimanded, holding up his glass and a pickle.

Sir picked up one of the green appetizers and motioned to Brie. "You should take a bite after you down the drink. It helps, trust me."

Brie picked up a small pickle and looked at it dubiously.

"*Za zdarov'ye!*" Rytsar toasted with a mischievous grin.

Sir held up his glass in response to the toast.

They both looked at her expectantly, so she held up her glass and smiled.

Both men exhaled deeply to one side and then threw back their heads and gulped the drink down. Brie was horrified and amazed to see them drink so much at once. Before they were finished she exhaled quickly and threw her head back. She struggled to take a gulp and then another to down the burning liquid. She was about to take a breath when Rytsar tipped the glass back up.

"Drink," he commanded with a wink.

With determination, she downed the entire glass, tears pricking her eyes as her whole nasal passage burned from the strong alcohol. "Eat," he said kindly, taking the glass from her and holding the pickle to her lips. She struggled not to cough as she took a small bite.

Rytsar grinned and smacked her on the back. "Well done, *radost moya!*" He immediately poured another glass for all three. Brie looked at Sir nervously.

Sir's smile was reassuring. "Russian tradition, little sub, but you can call your safe word."

"No!" Rytsar laughed. "*Radost moya* is no coward." He handed her back the glass with the same amount of liquid as the first time. The alcohol was already warming her entire body. It was an agreeable feeling, now she'd got past the initial unpleasantness.

She held up her glass to show her willing participation.

Sir nodded his approval and gave the next toast. "To all the pigheaded aristocrats in the world."

Rytsar looked properly insulted, but he and Brie clinked glasses.

It was just as much of a struggle as the first time, but she drank it all without any help. Afterwards, she took a big bite of the salty pickle and grinned at both men.

"You are now an honorary Russian," Rytsar proclaimed, giving her a spirited pat on the back that sent her tumbling into Sir's arms.

"Had enough?" her Master asked.

It took a few seconds to formulate the correct answer with all the warm yumminess coursing through her. "If it pleases you, Sir."

He put her glass down and answered, "It does, téa. I think you've had enough." He gave his own glass back to Rytsar. "I, however, would like another."

Rytsar gladly filled it up. "My turn for the toast."

Sir nodded with a grin. "You *are* the host."

Brie had expected to hear a witty insult. Instead Rytsar said, "To you, *moy droog*. You have seen me through great troubles."

Sir's face suddenly became solemn. "Same here, my friend." The men clinked glasses and downed their drinks, giving each other a heartfelt embrace afterwards. It was the most vulnerable Brie had seen Sir, other than with her. In that moment, she understood how close the two really were—like brothers.

Rytsar cleared his throat afterwards. "One more?" he asked, holding up the vodka bottle.

"No. I need to remain clear-headed," Sir replied.

Rather than giving Sir a hard time, Rytsar nodded and poured himself a drink, then downed it easily. He gave a satisfied sigh and smiled at Brie. "Nothing like vodka to open up the soul."

Brie giggled, flying on the warm cloud that was consuming her from the inside out.

"Come, Brie," Sir commanded. She looked over to see him sitting on the couch with his legs spread open.

As she approached Sir, she asked, "How would you like me, Master?"

He patted the area next to him. She giggled, finding it funny that he didn't want her between his legs. She gracefully sat down next to her Master. Sir told her to lay her head on his lap, and he began stroking her hair.

Rytsar joined them, sitting on the other side of Sir. He sighed loudly after he'd sat down. "I will miss you, peasant. It has been good to have you in my homeland."

Sir continued petting Brie's hair as he spoke. Tingles of electricity ran down her spine as his deep voice rumbled. "It is a shame it must end, Durov. This has reminded me of old times."

Rytsar chuckled. "*Da.*"

Brie closed her eyes and fell into the pleasant warmth of the vodka and the soothing feel of Sir's touch.

Her Master continued, "I can't imagine why I waited so long to visit."

"It's alright, idiot."

Brie giggled on Sir's lap. They definitely sounded like brothers.

"Did your sub just disrespect me?" Rytsar asked.

"I'm not sure." Sir lifted her chin. "Did you just disrespect my longtime friend, téa?"

Brie looked at him and smiled. "No, Sir. I respect your friend very much."

He smiled and cradled her face. "I suspected as much."

Rytsar huffed. "If giggling is a sign of respect, I need another drink." He got up and poured himself an additional glass.

The warm feeling coursing through Brie must have been coursing through Sir, because he suddenly changed positions, pulling her up and kissing her forcibly on the lips. "Undo my pants and grind on me," he growled huskily.

Brie quickly obeyed and straddled him so she was face to face with him. She eased her pussy over his cock and coated it with her slick excitement as she moved up and down the length of his shaft without taking him inside her. He grabbed her hips and helped to guide her movements.

"Your pussy is so beautiful, téa."

She felt warm butterflies stirring. "Thank you, Master."

"Let me inside."

Sir lifted her off, removing his clothes before positioning her pussy over his rigid cock again. She slowly guided his shaft into her, purring as she settled down fully on his manhood.

He threw his head back and groaned. "I love the feel of you."

She ground hard against him, needing him deeper. She was oblivious to the world as she made love to her Master...until she felt manly hands on her ass.

Sir leaned forward and whispered into her ear, "My gift to you."

Brie whimpered as she felt Rytsar's fingers explore the valley between her legs. A tingling chill coursed through her body at the thought she was about to DP with both men.

Sir caressed her cheek. "Normally, I like to be the one teasing your ass, but not this time." He kissed her on the lips before adding, "I want to look into your eyes today."

She caught her breath, his words having a physical effect on her.

"Such a sexy ass," Rytsar complimented. He kneaded her buttocks several times before inserting a lubricated finger into her anus.

Brie whimpered again. The thought of what was about to happen threatened to undo her.

"It's okay, little sub. We will start off gentle," Sir said, teasing her.

She moaned as Rytsar pressed his finger in farther. "She is extremely tight."

Sir gazed directly into Brie's eyes and smiled. "Don't worry, she loosens up with play." To Brie he said, "I know your desires, téa. Even those you are afraid to voice aloud. The two of us want to give this to you. It will be our first time as well, as he and I have never scened together like this before."

"Oh, Sir…" Brie whispered.

Rytsar asked in a husky voice, "Are you ready, *radost moya?*"

Brie closed her eyes and nodded.

Sir reprimanded her softly. "Open those pretty eyes."

She looked at Sir as the round head of Rytsar's cock pressed against her. *Breathe,* she reminded herself as he separated her buttocks and pushed a little harder.

"Open for him, téa," Sir commanded, before they locked lips.

She became lost in his kiss, but cried out when the head of Rytsar's cock breached her entrance. It stretched her achingly, but she found it immensely satisfying. The Russian grabbed a fistful of hair and pulled her head back as he held onto her waist with his other hand.

Sir stared up at her lustfully, watching her varying expressions as she accepted Rytsar inside her. Soft mews escaped her lips as her body struggled to take both men at once.

The Russian Dom leaned forward and bit her on the shoulder blade. Growling against her skin, he left a trail of bite-marks on her back. She cried out in passion and felt him thrust his shaft even deeper.

Sir wrapped his hand around the back of her neck, drawing her to him. "Deny us nothing, téa," he said, kissing her bottom lip.

"Yes, Master," she murmured breathlessly. Rytsar

started on her right shoulder blade, causing Brie to moan again.

"I want to feel my cock deep inside you, *radost moya.* I will pump my hot seed deep in this tight ass."

His dirty words had a positive effect as her body received another inch of his shaft. "More," she cried, but her body resisted farther advancement, despite her willingness.

Sir sneaked his hand down and smacked her on the butt. The sexy sound of it turned her on. "Again, Master," she begged.

"Make room," Sir told Rytsar as he wound up to spank her properly. The second stinging slap caused her to yelp in pleasure.

Rytsar's deep groan greeted their play as his cock sank all the way in. Brie felt chills as her body accepted the fullness of both men. She panted against Sir's chest, savoring the moment.

Sir gave her time to adjust before he seized her hips for leverage and pulled out so he could thrust back inside her. Rytsar waited to ascertain his rhythm before grabbing her waist and alternating his strokes. The men kept the rhythm slow but consistent, allowing her body to grow accustomed to the movement before they began fully thrusting inside her.

Brie screamed the first time they each gave a full stroke. It was almost too much. Sir kept his eyes on her. "Give in, *téa.*"

She closed her eyes as a tingling sensation grew from her core and slowly spread outwards.

"Good girl."

Brie opened her eyes for Sir and basked in the glory of receiving both cocks deeply. Pleasing both Doms at the same time was deliciously decadent—the ultimate fantasy.

Rytsar changed things up when he stopped thrusting and grabbed her by the shoulders, forcing her up so that her back was against his chest. He wrapped one hand around her throat and nibbled on her neck as he clasped her right breast possessively with his other hand. "My cock missed you, *radost moya.*"

Brie moaned, her body remembering quite well the last time he'd taken her.

Sir used the opportunity to rub his fingers vigorously against her clit. Her pussy was already on fire, engorged with fierce desire. She twitched in Rytsar's arms as Sir stoked the flames. She thrashed her head against the Russian's chest, a captive to the orgasm they were about to unleash.

She started screaming, unable to form coherent words. "Ah… Ahh…!"

Brie turned her head and bit down on Rytsar's wrist in desperation. He roared his approval, forcing his cock deep into her ass as his hand tightened around her neck. "Yes," he growled hoarsely. "Come for my cock, *radost moya.*"

She looked down at Sir, her whole body melting when she saw the intensity of his gaze—as if he could swallow her whole. He mouthed the words, "Come now."

It was a confusion of sensations as her pussy tried to contract but could not, being stretched unnaturally tight.

Instead, it became an intense burning that radiated from her pussy and blew through her. Her scream caught in her throat as her senses were blinded by the rush.

When she regained her awareness, she found herself staring down at Sir while Rytsar breathed low, haunting words into her ear, probably Russian—Brie was oblivious.

Rytsar let go of her and she returned her head to Sir's chest, reveling in the unique subspace they had evoked.

Brie purred, "Yes," when they started up again, thrusting deep into her body. She became a ravenous canvas for them, anxious to be transformed into something new by the two sexual artists.

Sir ordered her to cross her arms behind her. He then wrapped her in a tight embrace. "Fuck her," he commanded of Rytsar, while he remained still, buried in her quivering pussy.

Sir effectively became her bindings as he gave Rytsar free rein over her ass. Instead of pumping into her hard, he experimented with different angles. It took time until Rytsar found the one that made her shudder all over.

Being held captive by Sir was sexy on all kinds of levels. She listened to his heartbeat as Rytsar began stroking her at the perfect angle. Each thrust brought a symphony of pleasure. She reveled in the feeling, allowing it to carry her higher.

Rytsar grunted as she tensed. The sound of his lusty pleasure turned her on further. She felt her pussy start to pulse in time with her Master's heartbeat. She was sexually in sync with him, and the thought of it sent her to the edge.

"Master, I want to come for you."

"Yes, téa."

Tears of joy ran down Brie's cheeks as she lost herself. She heard the lustful releases of both men as they rocked her body with their orgasms, and then all became warm and silent. She floated higher, as if in a dream, the alcohol enhancing the natural high of her subspace.

When she felt Rytsar move, she protested. Sir chuckled beneath her. "All good things must come to an end, my little flyer."

It was with reluctance that she returned to earth as the lonely sound of a cell phone echoed in the other room.

Rytsar finally disengaged to answer it. He returned, holding the cell phone out to Sir.

Sir took it and answered in an official tone, not giving away the fact he was naked and buried inside his sub.

The person on the other end was speaking so fast, Brie could not make out what was said, but she grew concerned at Sir's serious expression. "We will be leaving in a few days. Surely, that will leave enough time." He paused again. "I'm afraid so."

Brie quietly detached herself from him, trying to conceal her worry.

When Sir finally ended the call, he surprised her by laughing.

"What's going on?" Rytsar demanded.

"Sorry, friend. I'm not allowed to speak of it. But I need to see if we can't get a flight out sooner."

He turned to Brie with a wistful look on his face. "Well, babygirl…it looks like your life is about to change."

His Pride

Rytsar was an influential man in Moscow, and was able to secure Brie and Sir a flight back to the States. On the drive to the airport, he complained, "I do not like this sudden leaving, *moy droog*. Nor the secrecy behind it."

Sir smirked. "Sorry, I was instructed not to divulge any information. You will know it as soon as Brie has permission to share."

Rytsar looked at her, defiance flashing in his eyes. "I had better be the first you inform, *radost moya*."

She opened her mouth, ready to assure him that he would be, but Sir interrupted. "Make no promises."

Brie suddenly became worried. *How serious is this secret?*

Rytsar frowned at Sir, sounding deeply offended. "I deserve to know."

Sir placed his hand on the Russian's shoulder. "There is no need to get your feathers ruffled, my friend. I simply think Brie will want to share it with others first. Rest assured, you will be told in a timely manner."

He growled in dissatisfaction. "I do not care to be left in the dark."

"It seems fitting you should suffer after your airport shenanigans. To abuse my sub in such a manner when she'd barely stepped onto Russian soil…"

"She handled herself fine, *moy droog*. You were the one who had me in stitches," said Rytsar, laughing.

Sir shrugged off the laughter at his expense. "Insulting me won't help your cause. Brie is capable of putting you farther down the list of people to call."

The Russian gave Brie a domineering look and barked, "Don't."

She struggled not to smile. It was humorous that the secret Sir was keeping was bothering Rytsar almost as much as it was bothering her.

Once they were safely on the plane, a private business jet with only a few prominent Russians on board, Sir shared the remarkable news with Brie. "Mr. Holloway has run into an unforeseen snag in his latest project. They are on a forced hiatus while it is being ironed out. His insistence on confidentiality is to prevent already gun-shy investors from backing out of his project before he has a chance to remedy the situation."

Brie stared at Sir, not really hearing anything after he mentioned the name 'Holloway'. Her heart began racing. *This is my big break!*

Sir continued, "He only has a few days, but said your documentary has been on his mind. He wants to see it in three days' time."

That was when reality hit. "Three days, Sir?"

"Yes. That's why I cut the trip short. You will basically have forty-eight hours, by the time we make it back to LA, to finish editing your documentary."

"It's not enough time," she protested.

"It *is* enough time," he corrected, "since it is all the time you've been given."

She bit back the feeling of panic and nodded. "Yes, Sir. I will make it work."

He covered her with a blanket. "Go to sleep, Brie," Sir commanded. "This will be the only chance you have for the next three days."

Obeying him was nearly impossible, but she forced herself to count sheep and then gave up on that, concentrating on Sir's breathing instead. It eased her into slumber—the reassuring force of his presence.

She had to fight back the thought that kept invading her head: *This is the beginning…*

Brie spent the next two days hunched over her computer, drinking coffee and eating apples at Sir's insistence—his idea of a more healthy energy booster. He took it upon himself to cook and care for her so that she could focus solely on editing the film.

Brie lived and breathed her documentary, from her first night at the Submissive Training Center to the last, when she, Lea and Mary had contemplated what the future held for them. She was obsessed with the last part of her footage, where both Lea and Mary had questioned her choice to be collared. At the time, she had only been considering Tono and Faelan, with no idea how the night would end up playing out.

However, it was difficult to listen to Mary. Brie had to fight back the bile rising in her throat when Mary mentioned wanting to take a spin with Faelan. Lea had jumped on her for it, but Brie had actually defended Mary. At the time she'd mistakenly thought the back-stabber was her friend.

It shocked Brie just how many times Mary had called her an idiot for wanting to get collared. Her claim that Brie just needed to 'play the field' in order to find better Doms had been a lie. The truth was that Mary hadn't wanted Brie to be happy at all, and had been willing to do whatever it took to prevent it.

Mary was the lowest, most spiteful person she knew. Brie's only consolation was that despite her nemesis' best efforts, Brie had still got her happy ending. Although graduation night hadn't gone the way she'd envisioned, the end result had been far better than Brie could ever have hoped for. It turned out that Mary's hatred had been unable to stop what was meant to be.

Brie imagined seeing Blonde Nemesis in a club someday and walking up to her just to say, "Thanks for being such a backstabbing bitch. I couldn't be happier because of you."

It was difficult not to cut Mary out of the film alto-gether. Just seeing her beautiful but stone-cold face brought back a flood of emotions. Her nemesis might have become a capable submissive, but she was a wretched excuse for a human being.

There was only one problem: Brie knew Mary added

to her documentary. Despite failing miserably as a friend, Blonde Nemesis was an 'interesting character'. That was how Brie had decided to think of her as she edited—just a two-dimensional character. To see Mary any other way only caused her pain.

Once Brie had selected the scenes she wanted, she spent the rest of the time finding and timing the music to match, as well as adding graphics and text. It wasn't going to be a polished piece of work by any means, but the meat of the story was well represented.

When she announced she was finished, Sir asked to watch it. "I want to see what you've been able to create." He sat down and pulled her to him, wrapping his arm around her waist. She'd missed his touch over the last two days in her mad rush to get the project completed, and was thrilled to feel that familiar electricity his touch evoked.

Brie was nervous when she hit play. She tried not to be obvious as she observed his reactions while he watched the film. Her heart soared whenever he smiled, but she saw the look of genuine concern when Brie spoke of the incident between Mary and Tono.

Because Brie hadn't become friends with her yet, it was simply Brie's impressions of the evening Blonde Nemesis had flipped out. The girl had been purchased by Tono at an auction, but had had a psychological break-down in his care because of her failure to disclose her serious underlying issues.

Brie was surprised to see Sir's smile return when Lea questioned Brie about her Kinbaku experience with Tono. Brie had been flying high after such an incredible and unusual bondage session with the talented Dom. It was apparent she'd fallen for Tono that night by her actions and words, despite Brie's attempts to edit. She had wanted to avoid hurting Sir, but had remained true to the documentary.

Sir maintained that smile when, later in the film, she shared with the other two girls about her day with Faelan after he'd won her at the auction. The only times she saw Sir twitch uncomfortably were when she talked about her growing feelings for Sir himself.

When the credits rolled across the screen she turned it off, but was startled by his silence. Finally, Sir turned to her and said, "This is a telling piece."

She smiled uncertainly. "Do you feel it is worthy of distribution?"

"You have done a fine job depicting your journey as a submissive...the insecurities, triumphs and eventual growth. Your humor is a nice touch."

She blushed at the compliment, but she still wanted to know. "Thank you, Sir. But...do you like it?"

He touched her cheek lightly. "Your raw honesty in the film has given me new understanding of your personal journey. I hope you are prepared for the exposure, Brie. You are quite open in this film. There are many people who do not understand the lifestyle and will attack you for it."

"I've taken that under serious consideration, Sir. I fully accept what will come because of this film."

He tilted his head slightly. "Even with your own parents?"

She sighed, hating the thought of it. "Yes, Sir. I am

willing to face anyone who does not understand."

He stood up and walked to the expansive window overlooking the city.

She stayed where she was, very aware that he had not answered her question—not directly—so she quietly asked it one more time. "Sir, did you like it?"

He held out his hand. She instantly got up and approached him, then knelt at his feet. He put his hand on the top of her head. "I admire this piece of work you have created. However, I cannot say 'like' is a word I would use. I can foresee that this will subject you and the other two girls to unnecessary strife." He helped her onto her feet. "That being said, considering how much time you've had to edit it, I find it an exceptional piece of work."

She wrapped her arms around him. "Thank you, Sir. It means so much to me to hear you say that."

He lifted her chin to look into her eyes. "No matter how this affects our lives, I am proud to stand with you in this moment."

I love this man!

Brie stood on her tiptoes to kiss him. "I'm truly honored, Sir."

He grasped the back of her neck and kissed her deeply. "I believe we both need to connect on a more intimate level."

Brie's heart leapt with joy. "I've missed your touch these last few days, Master."

"As have I. Undress and kneel by the Tantra chair while I select a new tool for you."

She felt weak inside as she removed her clothes and

folded them neatly by her feet. Brie walked over to the lounger and knelt beside it, waiting for his return. In mere seconds, she'd gone from a tired filmmaker to a willing submissive. It was a glorious transition.

Sir was naked when he walked back into the room, his strides confident and lithe like those of a predator. He held only a spreader bar, but this was different from the previous one he had used on her. This bar had *four* cuffs on it.

"Today you learn a favorite Kama Sutra position of mine, téa."

"It is my pleasure to do so, Master."

"It is challenging in its depth."

Brie moaned softly, the thought of it making her loins ache with pleasure.

Sir placed the bar on the floor and asked her to stand before it. He buckled each ankle to an outer cuff, the bar forcing her legs apart. Then he commanded, "Give me your left wrist."

Brie bent down and Sir secured her wrist to the middle of the bar. He took her right wrist and did the same, leaving Brie standing with her legs straight, her head between her knees and her ass in the air.

He stood up and moved behind her to admire the view. "Your ass is a piece of art, woman."

Sir rubbed his hands over her buttocks and down her back. Brie glanced at the window to stare at her reflection. It was a defenseless pose, leaving her completely open to Master's whims.

"I see your pussy is swollen with desire, téa." He spanked her mound lightly, sending bursts of sensual electricity to her core. Her nipples hardened in response. He slapped it again with a little more enthusiasm, making her whimper with pleasure.

"Your pussy has missed its Master."

"Yes, Master. It's desperate for you."

He caressed her ass again, squeezing and releasing the flesh, randomly patting her mound when the urge struck. Brie struggled to keep her balance as he played with her.

Sir ran his finger over her wet slit and commented, "You appear ready." Instead of plowing into her, he walked into the kitchen. She heard him take down a glass and make himself a martini.

He knew exactly how to play her mind and body. Waiting for his attention in this suggestive pose was extremely effective. She glanced at the window again and smiled.

Sir walked back in several minutes later and stood beside her, sipping his martini. "The position is called the Second Posture, but I modify it slightly for the added benefit the chair provides. It requires flexibility and arousal to accomplish. Are you aroused, téa?"

"Yes, Master."

"Remember this position, as I plan to use it often." Sir put down his drink before he slipped his arm under her stomach. Brie squealed when he lifted her off the ground. She felt like a sexy sack of potatoes, completely at the mercy of the man who carried her.

He deftly laid her on her back, the Tantra chair cradling her body with its gentle curvature.

Brie relaxed in the chair, but Sir instructed, "Legs

straight up."

Brie obeyed and watched in excitement as Sir strad-dled the chair and sat facing her, his cock resting on her bare mound. He grabbed the bar and pushed her legs towards her head, lifting her buttocks off the chair and her pussy at an inviting angle to receive his manhood.

Sir smiled as he slid his shaft into her and pressed his torso against her legs, still holding onto the bar with one hand. Brie let out a gasp as he thrust deeper, the angle of the chair and his position demanding that she relax in a major way.

He rolled his hips slowly, allowing her body to ap-preciate every inch of his shaft as he slid in and out. It was a challenge to take him this way, but with her legs straight the position was particularly stimulating to her G-spot. He gazed down at her and whispered huskily, "This is just the beginning."

Sir pressed harder against the bar, forcing her legs farther back, nearer to her head. She commanded her muscles to loosen and accept the awkward position as Sir gained deeper access.

"It becomes less about the thrusting and more about the depth as you relax, téa," he said huskily. Brie had been concentrating on relaxing her muscles and had failed to notice the look of ecstasy on her Master's face until now.

She smiled up at him, encouraging him to push the bar farther. With his patience and her willingness, he eventually pushed her legs all the way back until her feet and wrists were next to her head. Sir stopped thrusting and held onto the bar with both hands, looking down at her with a mixture of love and passion.

He pulled out and then slowly pressed his cock back in, letting her body embrace his fullness to the very base of his manhood. Then he began rocking back and forth—the head of his hard shaft in constant contact with her G-spot, rubbing it heatedly. "My cock cherishes you as much as I do, téa."

She nodded, unable to speak due to the demanding position.

"Let it love you to release."

Her eyes focused solely on his as she felt the tingles and chills caused by the deep stimulation. Her nipples almost hurt, they had constricted so tightly, while tiny goosebumps rose on her skin. She was a captive of his love in every sense of the word as the buildup reached its crescendo and she gave in to the feeling. Her pussy caressed his cock in rhythmic adulation.

Sir stared down at her. "I love you," he said as his cock joined in the dance, releasing his seed deep inside her.

Hearts and bodies connected as one…

Sir gently pulled away, easing her legs down and un-buckling her from the spreader bar. He let it drop to the floor and gathered her in his arms, pressing her head against his shoulder. The gesture was so tender, so moving that Brie began to cry. He seemed to understand and did not question her or ask her to stop.

"Forever," she whispered.

Dreams Deferred

B rie stood before Mr. Holloway, confident that her documentary would wow him. The fact he had called her in to see it spoke of his vested interest in the project.

"Please, Miss Bennett, take a seat," he said in a firm, manly tone.

Brie looked him in the eye as she gracefully sat down. Sir had instructed her to treat the producer the way she would any business contact, despite the fact he was a known Dom.

She smiled amiably. "Thank you for offering to see my work, Mr. Holloway."

"Marquis Gray spoke highly of you and believed your work would reflect the same level of excellence he has come to expect from you in other areas."

Brie felt heat rise to her face, honored that he felt that way. "I hope I can do justice not only to his confidence in my abilities, but to the Training Center itself. It has changed my life, in ways I could never have imagined."

"Let's waste no more time then," he said affably.

Brie handed over the documentary—her baby—without hesitation. She watched him slip the DVD in and hit play. The large TV screen lit up with her introduction. The music started off light and soothing as the words 'Art of Submission' floated across the screen with images of submissives bowing, presenting, or kissing the hands or feet of the dominants. The music quickly became hard and pounding as more provocative images flashed onto the screen, depicting bondage, flogging and fire play.

Brie had ended the intro with pictures of the three girls with their silly nicknames: 'Lea the Lovely', 'Brie the Bodacious' and 'Mary the Magnificent'. She'd decided to keep the humor of their experiences at the forefront of her film. Becoming a submissive was a complex journey—one that not only involved facing fears and pushing limits, but also encouraged the pure joy of self-discovery.

She watched Mr. Holloway clandestinely as he took in her work. The man had his hand on his chin. His gaze never wavered; his lips never twitched. He was a master at masking his emotions. When the ending credits concluded, he turned off the TV and sat without saying a word.

With all her dreams on the line, such treatment should have put her in a tailspin of anxiety, but she knew it was good and stared back at him pleasantly, saying nothing. After several long, agonizing moments he spoke.

"It was not what I was expecting."

Brie swallowed hard, shocked by his reaction, but she kept her composure. "What was your expectation?"

"I had hoped for a more in-depth exposé of your training experience. That girl, Mary—you hardly touched on her issues and you left the end nebulous concerning her future. You also concentrated more on Lea's humor than her personal struggles. The only person I feel I know after watching your film is you, which is not bad…however, you have other personalities in the film who were not tapped into."

She took a deep breath before replying. "You are correct. I did not dig deeply into their personal lives. I didn't want to infringe on their privacy, especially with Mary, who has painful issues in her past."

"It is those issues that will make this film interesting. We need to know their pain and discomfort, just as you shared some of yours."

"I doubt they'd want to expose themselves like that, Mr. Holloway. Their willingness to publicly identify themselves as submissives was courageous enough. I am prepared to risk full exposure, but I do not expect the same from my friends."

"Well, you do not have a noteworthy film without it. You need more footage, individual interviews in which you delve into the darker aspects of their journeys. In fact, I would wager even you have held back some of your more difficult trials."

Brie nodded. "You are correct again. I consciously made the decision not to burden the viewer."

"Then it is not really a documentary, is it? It is a piece of well-packaged fluff. I expected a documentary, and *that* I did not get."

Brie took a deep breath and exhaled silently before speaking, grateful for Tono's breathing lessons at a time like this. "I thank you for your time, Mr. Holloway." She got up to leave, completely devastated but hiding it under a pleasant smile.

He motioned her back to the chair. "I want my documentary, Miss Bennett. Go back to Ms. Taylor and Miss Wilson and get their real stories. Go to the Training Center and video some of the scenes you allude to. I would also like to see interviews with the trainers. This film has potential, but not as it is now."

"I am fairly certain I will not get the consent of both submissives. I had a hard enough time getting what little I did get from the one."

"Miss Wilson?"

"Yes," she answered.

"It is her story that will sell the film. I don't care what you have to do, it is imperative you get her to agree."

"We did not end on good terms, Mr. Holloway."

He smiled wolfishly. "All the better."

"And if I cannot get her consent?"

He sat back slowly in his chair. "Then you don't have a film, in my opinion."

Brie's heart dropped. There was no way Mary would agree—not the Blonde Nemesis. "I will see what I can do. How soon do you want the completed film?"

"In a month."

She shook her head to clear it. A month was not a reasonable amount of time for all he wanted her to add to the documentary. However, this man was her best chance and she wasn't about to question him on it. "Shall we set up a meeting for in a month, then?"

He gave her a look of approval. "Had you made any excuses, I would have turned down the project. You may see my assistant on the way out to schedule our next meeting." The imposing man stood up and handed back the DVD. "I expect great things from you, Miss Bennett."

She took it with a feeling of disappointment, sad that her little film had failed to impress him. *What will Sir say?*

She nodded to the respected producer and headed for the door.

"I like your sense of humor, Miss Bennett. Do not lose that in the remake. You'll need the balance."

She turned around and smiled. "Thank you, Mr. Holloway. I find humor makes everything easier to digest."

Brie walked out of the building and got into her car, feeling shell-shocked. He had not rejected the film, but it felt like it—especially knowing that Mary was the key. She rested her head on the steering wheel and closed her eyes. That was not how she'd thought the meeting would go, and now she would have to go back to Sir and tell him her film wasn't good enough.

She jumped when someone knocked on her driver-side window. Brie looked up and saw Sir staring down at her. He made the motion for her to roll down the window. "I wanted to be the first to congratulate you."

Her bottom lip trembled.

Sir paused for a second and then smiled. "Let's go for a walk, babygirl."

Brie got out of the car and Sir placed his hand on the small of her back, guiding her through the crowds of people hustling down the sidewalk. His touch brought welcome peace to her soul.

"How did it go?" he asked gently. "I can tell by your body language and silence that you aren't happy, but I can't imagine he rejected it."

She struggled to talk without her emotions choking her voice. "Mr. Holloway rejected what I have now."

"But…"

"If I can get Mary's and Lea's consent to do more personal interviews, along with a host of other things within a month's time, he'll accept it. Well…he'll consider it, at least. But Mary will never agree to it, Sir. It's done." She held back a sob and turned away from him.

Sir directed her to a ledge so that she could sit down. He stood over her, allowing her time to collect herself. "I understand your disappointment, Brie. However, the door has not been closed. He is providing you with an excellent opportunity. It is not over—this is just the beginning."

Brie looked up at Sir, unable to hide her misery. "The last thing I want is to talk to Mary again, much less ask a favor of her, Sir. To realize my dream I have to face my worst nightmare."

"I take it as a good sign. The unresolved issues between you two need to be addressed. It seems the universe agrees and is forcing the issue."

"Anything but that…" she whimpered.

He said quietly, "You are no longer a child."

It was humiliating to be put in this position. Mary

had wronged her, Mary was the one at fault, but it was Brie who was expected to mend the rift the betrayer had created.

"Brie, let me give you a piece of advice, one I learned after my father's death. No matter how it may appear to the casual observer, you cannot know the truth unless you know all sides. I would refrain from making judgments until you speak with Miss Wilson directly."

Brie bowed her head. *Yes, Sir knows too well the cost of unjust judgments.* His words brought clarity in a sea of doubt and frustration. "I'll speak to her, Sir. But I already know it's going to end in disaster."

Sir chuckled. "I doubt that. I remember seeing the two of you together. There were times of honest camaraderie between you. Don't be so quick to dismiss that because of one incident you have yet to discuss."

"You have more faith in her than I do, Sir."

"My faith lies in you, Brie."

She stood up and wrapped her arms around his waist. "Thank you, Sir. I needed to hear that."

His strong arms embraced her and he lifted her off the ground. "You are meant to accomplish great things. To whom much is given, much is expected." He kissed her firmly on the lips.

Brie melted into his kiss, and laid her head against his chest when he set her back down. "As long as I have you, I know I can't fail."

He squeezed her tighter. "I have news of my own, little sub."

Brie looked up and smiled. "What is it, Sir?"

"One of the business contacts I made in Russia has

plans for expansion into America. They've asked to meet in New York."

She was genuinely pleased. "Your dreams of expanding your business are coming true, Sir."

"Like yours, they are not happening the way I anticipated, and yet a unique opportunity has presented itself." He traced the collar fastened around her neck and added with a charming smile, "I believe you are my luck."

His words warmed her heart in ways he could not imagine. For a man who'd struggled in the past to communicate his feelings, Sir was becoming exceptionally expressive.

She squeezed him tighter. "I'm thrilled to hear it, Sir."

"There is a hitch, however. They are meeting later this week. I'll need to leave tomorrow to get my contacts set up and presentation ready."

A cold shiver of realization ran through her. "Will I be going with you, Sir?"

"No, Brie. You don't have time to spare on another trip. I regret that I cannot be here as support."

She sat back down on the ledge, trying to keep the tears of disappointment at bay. Brie thought what a funny creature she was—one moment flying high, and the next drowning in despair.

"Brie, do not let this deter you from your goal. Even when I am not near, my love and support are yours."

He'd said the L word in public without a second thought, his concern for her so great that he wasn't even aware of it. That one word changed everything in an instant.

She looked up at him, trying not to smile foolishly. "I won't, Sir. Although I wish you could be here if the meeting with Mary does not go well."

Always thinking ahead, Sir immediately suggested, "You should take Ms. Taylor with you and present the opportunity to the two at the same time. If Miss Wilson is not receptive, leave with Ms. Taylor. She can act as your moral support and a buffer if you require it."

Brie nodded, her confidence returning. With her best friend Lea by her side, she could face the Nemesis. Only Lea truly knew the trials she had suffered with Mary, anyway.

"I'd say we are both due a lavish night of celebration, Miss Bennett. Perhaps a quiet Italian dinner by the ocean and a ride along the coast."

She looked at him demurely. "Whatever is your pleasure, Sir."

"You are my pleasure, téa," he said, gathering her back into his arms.

Sir told Brie to pick out an outfit he would like, but added the stipulation there were to be no bra or panties involved. Brie walked into their closet, her eyes widening at the choices. Sir had purchased several outfits she had yet to wear and they were exquisite—and yet…

Brie walked out of the bedroom with a confident stride that spoke of her assurance as a cherished submissive. When Sir saw her, there was a slight moment of obvious surprise, and then his lips curled upwards in pleasure.

"My student."

Brie glided up to him dressed in her Submissive Training uniform: the leather corset, short skirt and her thigh-highs with six-inch heels. Tonight, per his request, she had forgone the red thong underneath.

"Are you pleased, Master?"

He kissed her in answer, reaching under her leather skirt. Brie ground against his hand. Sir licked his finger afterwards, smiling sensually before picking up a velvet box from the counter.

Inside were the pearls that he'd given Brie the night he'd scened with her as 'Khan'. Sir placed the strand around her neck, letting it hang between her breasts. "Perfection, téa."

Sir went to get dressed himself and left her with the instructions, "While you wait, I want you to come up with a use for those pearls tonight."

Brie played with the pearls around her neck, a sly smile forming on her lips. She knew *exactly* how she would use them.

It was her turn to look surprised when he came back out. He was dressed in the same tux he'd worn the night he'd collared her. Seeing him walk towards her in the black Italian suit made her knees weak. "You look beautiful, Sir."

He cocked his head. "Beautiful? That's not a word I hear often." He chuckled as he took her evening coat from the hook in the hallway and slipped it over her shoulders. Sir whispered in her ear, "Still my elegant property."

Brie purred. When she had played out the scene with Sir as her Khan, it had been exciting but full of emotional angst. This time the barriers were gone; she was simply a devoted sub in the hands of her Master.

"I love you, Master."

He cupped her chin. "I don't think you know the depth of my feelings for you."

Chills ran down her spine as she looked into his eyes. Unlike Marquis' gaze that bored into her soul, Sir's called to her like a perilous song, inviting her to lose herself completely.

He walked her out of the building to a waiting limousine. She smiled and pressed herself against him as they waited for the chauffeur to open the door. Brie remembered the last limousine ride, one that had been full of passion but had ended in utter frustration.

Not tonight…

Brie slid onto the long, leather bench seat, feeling lightheaded with expectation. Sir joined her, putting his hand on her thigh, but he remained silent. For the entire ride he did not speak. He simply stared at her with a look of longing and some unknown emotion—an almost raw vulnerability. It reminded her of their first time alone together.

Her heart started to race. What could it mean? She met his gaze, asking silently, *What are you trying to tell me, Sir?*

The limo stopped on the coast at a quiet area of beach. Sir helped her out of the car and escorted her towards the water on a path of red tiles that had been laid out artfully for them. The footpath led to a lone table in the sand, surrounded by fiery tiki torches. A man dressed like a chef stood with a chair pulled out for her.

Brie smiled. "What's this, Master?"

"A quiet Italian meal by the ocean," he replied.

Brie sat down at the elegantly set table and stared across it as her Master sat down. This was too much—something extraordinary was happening tonight. She could feel it in her bones.

The chef removed covers from two plates, one with small grilled pieces of bread, and the other with colorful vegetables and a small bowl of oil. Sir pointed to the bread. "*Fettunta*, spread with olive oil, grilled with garlic rubbed on top. Best garlic bread you'll ever taste." He pointed to the other. "*Pinizimonio*, fresh vegetables to dip in the seasoned olive oil."

"It looks delicious, Master."

Sir picked up a slice of bread and consumed it with a look of rapture on his face. Brie was captivated by the vibrant vegetables and took a slice of bright yellow bell pepper, dipping it into the olive oil seasoned with black pepper. She brought it to her lips, trying to look alluring. A drip of oil fell before she could get it into her mouth. It landed on her chest, then rolled slowly under her corset and between her breasts. She looked up, hoping Sir hadn't noticed. The twinkle in his eyes said otherwise.

"Take off your top, téa."

Brie ignored the stranger standing beside her and undid the ties, letting her corset fall to the sandy beach. Sir stood up and with his finger, he caught the trail of oil. He lifted his index finger to his lips and licked it off. "I think you would taste good covered in olive oil."

He sat back down and took a mushroom, dipping it into the oil. Then, smiling at Brie, he devoured it. She blushed. Sir could eat her any way he wanted...

The chef poured them each a glass of wine, before moving back to a grill she hadn't noticed flaming in the distance until now. Sir was right—her favorite, hands down, was the garlic bread; hard, crunchy, infused with the taste of garlic and the tanginess of olive oil. She had to stop herself from eating the whole plateful. *Submissives are not greedy*, she reminded herself, *even if they secretly want to be*.

After several minutes, the chef returned with a covered plate. He placed it before Sir and lifted the cover with a flourish. A thick, juicy steak sat alone on the platter. It was not the pasta Brie had expected.

Sir took the knife the chef handed him and cut into it at an angle. Brie was shocked at how red it was, like rare—*really* rare.

He speared the piece of meat and held it up to admire. "*Bistecca alla Fiorentina*. A simple dish that impresses the most discerning palate."

Sir held it out for her to eat, but she did not open her lips to take it. With trepidation, she admitted, "I don't eat rare meat, Master."

He shook his head. "You have not tried this. Trust me, téa."

She opened her mouth, but only to please him, even though she was certain she would choke on it.

"It is seasoned simply and grilled only for a few minutes on each side, to let the true flavor of the beef shine through," he said as he put it in her mouth.

Brie let the bloody meat touch her lips and held back the urge to gag. Sir was watching her intently as she chewed, so she closed her eyes to concentrate on the flavors, divorcing herself from the fact it was basically raw animal tissue. The simple salt, pepper and garlic seasoning, along with the splash of olive oil, heightened the flavor of the steak. This meat *definitely* had flavor, but it was delicate and melted in her mouth.

She opened her eyes after she'd swallowed the enticing morsel. "Delicious."

Sir sat back with a satisfied grin. "Of course."

The chef took the knife from Sir and cut the rest of the meat into thin slices, then added a small bowl of white beans to the table.

"Is it to your liking, Sir Davis?" he asked.

"It is an excellent piece of meat. Thank you for the entire meal, Chef Sabello."

"My pleasure. I would do anything for the son of Alonzo."

Sir nodded gratefully.

Chef Sabello poured the last of the wine, made a small bow and walked into the darkness, leaving them alone on the secluded beach.

Sir scooped up a forkful of beans and said, "*Fagioli bianchi* are a bit like your mashed potatoes, a required accompaniment of the meal."

Brie took her own forkful of white beans to taste. Like everything else she had eaten that night, it was simple. A little bit of salt, oil and garlic, with a savory herb she couldn't identify. The simplicity of it made the ingredients stand out all the more.

"I love everything about this meal, Master. I've never had anything like it."

He chuckled. "Yes, I'm sure you were expecting pasta, possibly a meatball or two."

Brie giggled, instantly thinking of the animated movie *Lady and the Tramp*, when the two dogs shared the long noodle. She smiled bashfully at Sir as she imagined his lips coming closer to hers as they ate the single noodle from both ends.

Instead, she shared the same piece of mouthwatering meat and bowl of white beans with her Master. It was all the more wonderful because this meal had been a part of his childhood, something he desired to share with her.

Before they'd finished, Brie noticed a change come over Sir. He became quiet again. She could barely get her last mouthful down, wondering what was about to happen—not allowing herself to dream.

"I value sharing this with you, téa. This is a part of my past, the foods I grew up on. It pleases me that you enjoy them."

"I am honored you want to share them with me, Master."

"There are other things I long to share."

Brie's heartbeat increased. She got up from the table and walked over to him, kneeling down at his feet. "I cherish your trust in me…"—she almost said 'Thane', but chickened out—"…Master." She kissed the back of his hand in reverence.

He petted her head with his other hand. Sir cleared his throat, but did not speak. She felt an aura of tension radiating from him that was delightfully disconcerting. Her body responded by trembling with expectancy.

"Master?" she asked, looking up at him.

He smiled briefly, but shook his head. "No. Not yet… I think it's time we took a drive." Sir got up from the table and commanded, "Gather your top, téa. No need to dress."

Brie felt wistful leaving the romantic meal behind, already treasuring the memories. She returned to the limo bare-chested. The chauffeur did not bat an eyelid as he opened the door for them.

Pearls in the Sand

O nce again Sir sat next to Brie, his masculine hand on her thigh. But this time his need filled the small space. His fingers traveled upwards, tantalizingly slow in their progress, centimeter by aching centimeter.

Brie quivered under his touch, her breaths becoming rapid and shallow. Ever closer to her sweet spot he came, as his warm breath caressed her neck. His hand moved under her skirt, so close… A small cry escaped her lips when his finger finally touched the soft folds of her pussy. He kissed her neck as he made quick work of her excited clit. Soon she was grinding against his hand. His lips moved down to her nipple and he began sucking as his fingers progressed to her opening. With the same drawn-out playfulness, he teased her, rimming the entrance but not providing penetration. She whimpered in need.

Sir's lips moved up to her ear. "What do you want, Brie?"

"I need you, Sir. I need you inside me."

With the cruelty of a good Master, he pulled away

and sat back in the seat. "Not yet. You need to learn patience, sub."

She wanted to groan in frustration, but kept silent. *You want me, Sir. Take your willing sub.*

He shook his head, as if he could hear her thoughts. But he soon moved over to the window separating them from the driver and knocked on the glass. It slid down and he told the chauffeur, "This is the place coming up."

The driver turned the limo around and parked on the side of the road next to the coastline. Sir opened the car door and helped her out himself. Brie was still topless, but he wrapped his arm around her so that she was not exposed as he helped her down a path to a small beach surrounded by protruding rocks. She struggled to traverse the rocky path in her heels, so Sir picked her up and carried her. "I'm curious, téa. How will you use the pearls tonight?"

"It's a surprise, Master."

A lustful grin spread across his face. "I see."

When they'd reached the private alcove at the bottom, he set her down and played with the pearls around her neck. "Much like you, I struggle with surprises."

She looked up at him, smiling seductively. "Would you like me to show you then, Master?"

"Yes, your Master would like to see your use of pearls, téa."

She dropped to the hard-packed sand and began by taking off his shoes and socks. Then she relieved him of his slacks, pulling his briefs down along with them. She stood back up, undid his tie and unbuttoned his shirt. Sir sloughed off both his jacket and shirt, so that he stood completely naked before her.

Brie slowly gyrated to the rhythm of the ocean waves as she rid herself of her remaining clothes, so that she too was *au naturel*. He reached out for her and she moved into his embrace. Brie closed her eyes as she laid her head against his warm chest.

"My goddess," he murmured.

Brie looked up at him and smiled. "Would you please lie down on your back, Master, so that I may show you my pearls?"

Sir lay down on the ground, his eyes never leaving her. Brie knelt beside him and ran the pearls between her lips, looking at him suggestively before taking them off. With slow, sensuous movements, she lightly caressed his skin with the smooth pearls, causing goosebumps to appear. She concentrated on his chest first, but twirled the pearls lower and lower, towards his pelvic region. Just as they were about to touch his hardening cock, she reached down to his feet and started upward.

He groaned in lustful frustration as she teased him as cruelly as he had teased her. As she moved up to his thighs, she bent over and allowed her nipple to 'accidentally' graze his cock. It twitched in response to the brief contact.

She wanted his cock coated in her juices before she began, so she curled the pearls into a spiral circle over his bellybutton. "For safekeeping," she said with a smile, before standing up and turning so she was facing away from him. She straddled his hips and wiggled her ass seductively, before slowly lowering herself. She knew she was giving Sir a fine view of her ass in the moonlight.

He took hold of his cock so that it was waiting for her. Brie pressed against the tip of his hard shaft and then lowered herself all the way to its base before pulling up again. She looked behind her and asked, "Does Master like?"

He growled and grabbed both ass cheeks, forcing her back down in answer. Brie rode his shaft, enjoying the angle of the position and the control she had over his cock—when he allowed it. Once he was properly coated, she lifted herself off his shaft and settled down between his legs. She picked up the pearls and began slowly wrapping his cock in them.

Then she held onto them with both hands and began stroking him with the numerous round beads. Sir tilted his head back and closed his eyes—a good sign.

Brie rolled the pearls up and down his shaft, kissing and licking the head of his manhood as she did so.

"Harder," Sir groaned.

She pressed her hands together for more friction, adding a twisting motion to her movement. He stiffened underneath her, making Brie purr with excitement.

"Teeth."

She grazed the ridge of his shaft with her teeth, being careful not to bite down too hard. Sir shifted and she knew he was close. She moaned loudly, as excited as he.

Sir shuddered. He grunted as his hips thrust forward and his come filled her mouth. Brie pumped his cock in rhythm with his thrusts, eagerly swallowing her Master's essence. He grabbed her head as he guided her mouth for the last couple of surges, and then he held her still as his body shuddered one final time.

When he let Brie go, he pulled her onto his chest and wrapped his arms around her. She lay in his arms for several minutes. She listened to both his rapid heartbeat and the crashing of the ocean waves in the background. His hands ran down her back, caressing her skin with their electric touch, and then they suddenly stopped.

"Brie."

She lay still, holding her breath.

"You know that my feelings for you run deep."

"As do mine, Sir."

"How deep?" he asked. She lifted her head and saw that he was smiling.

"I love you more than life itself."

He instantly stiffened and his eyes clouded over with pain. Somehow, in declaring her love she had said something wrong. The look of torment on his face spoke of old wounds having been ripped wide open.

"Thane, I love you!" she said in desperation, not wanting to lose their intimacy.

He just stared at her as if he was seeing someone else.

She could feel Sir pulling away from her emotionally, almost as if it were a physical separation. "I don't understand," she cried. "Help me to understand, Sir."

When he spoke, his voice was calm but strained. "Get dressed."

She untangled herself from his embrace and put her clothes on, tears streaming down her face. Had her allusion to death hit a raw nerve? Could that simple error have been enough to upset him this profoundly? It didn't make sense, but he gave no reason for his hurtful behavior.

She went to pick up her strand of pearls lying in the sand, but he said, "Leave them."

They walked back to the limo in deathly silence.

"Put your corset on," he told her once inside the limousine, before turning his head and looking out of the window.

The ride home was every bit as uncomfortable as the end of their first limo ride had been. When they finally pulled up to the high rise, Sir instructed, "Go to bed. I don't expect to return until much later."

When her tears started up again, he closed his eyes and added, "I will explain...later."

The chauffeur opened the limousine door and Brie obediently left, although inside her heart was breaking.

A staff member opened the lobby door for her with a broad smile as the limousine pulled away. As she walked inside, Brie snarled under her breath. *I fucking hate limos!*

Sir did not return until dawn. Brie had been up all night waiting for him. It took everything in her not to run to confront him. Instead she lay curled up on the bed, her eyes swollen from crying.

He entered the bedroom and quietly undressed before joining her in bed. "I assume you got no sleep."

"No sleep, Sir."

He pulled her to him in a spoon position. "We both

need to rest. Close your eyes, téa."

Sir offered no explanation, but just having him beside her, wanting her near, was enough to quell her questions for now. She did as he asked and closed her eyes, giving in to a troubled sleep.

It wasn't until hours later that Sir stirred. Brie turned towards him and simply said, "Sir?"

He brushed her cheek lightly. "You said something, Brie…something my mother used to say to my father. You couldn't have known. I do not blame you."

She wanted to speak, but he put his finger to her lips.

"I told you once that I am undecided about fate. I do not know if your words are meant as a warning or a challenge to me."

She shook her head in protest.

He leaned forward and kissed her on the forehead. "I am taking it as a challenge. I have never dealt with my past. You are forcing me to face it straight on."

When Sir took his finger from her lips, she told him, "I didn't mean to hurt you, Sir."

"I know. It was said in love, but what are the chances you would answer with her words?"

"I would *never* hurt you in that way, Sir," she declared passionately.

"And that is where the quandary lies, for I am certain my mother would have said the same thing in the beginning."

Brie was hurt that he was comparing her to his mother—hinting that she would end up betraying him. She tried to pull away, but Sir grasped her arm. "Brie, in my head I know you are not the same, but right now…"

He let go then, and turned away from her.

With fear and trepidation, she asked, "Sir, what are you saying?"

Sir looked back at her, the expression on his face uncharacteristically open and unguarded. "Time. I need time, Brie."

She caressed his masculine jaw, rough with stubble. Smiling through her tears, Brie answered, "Sir, we are condors. We have a lifetime to find our way."

Animal Sex

Sir made Brie stay at home when he left for the airport later that day. He claimed he didn't want her to waste a single minute away from her project. "Look through what you already have that you can use to enhance your film. Decide what questions you want to ask both girls. You will need to be prepared before you approach Miss Wilson. You will also need to get permission from the Training Center for those extra shots the producer wanted. There is far too much for you to do to be wasting time at the airport seeing me off."

She nodded her agreement, but deep down inside she felt he was running away from her.

The second the door shut, life seemed to leave the entire apartment. It felt as if a part of her soul had left with him.

"Pull yourself together, Brie. You're not a weak-minded little girl who can't exist without her man."

She spent the night going back over her documentary footage. She concentrated on Mary, wanting to see if there was anything she could pull from it. She came across the moment when Mary had broken down in front of the camera, demanding she turn it off. Brie had been in the middle of giving her a compliment. In an instant, Mary's countenance had changed and she'd become hostile. Brie replayed it several times, zooming in on the girl's face. She swore she could see a look of longing in Mary's eyes, just before the walls came crashing down and the girl flipped out.

Maybe Sir was right. It was possible Mary was not a back-stabbing bitch. Well…not *only* a back-stabbing bitch.

As she was readying herself for bed, she was surprised to see the velvet box on the dresser. Curious, she opened it and gasped, clutching the sandy pearls to her chest. Sir had gone back for them…

She slipped under the covers wearing only the pearls. Unfortunately, the large bed only reminded her that he was gone. She curled up on his side of the bed and breathed in Sir's smell on his pillow. It was comforting and helped her to fall asleep. Brie knew it would be a long week ahead without him, but she had been an independent person before. There was no reason she couldn't survive—no, *thrive*—on her own.

She was sure the time apart would only help to make their reunion that much more passionate, if that were even possible.

He held out his hand and helped her out of the Mustang,

then slammed the car door in his haste. She could feel the animal lust radiating from her Master. He wanted her, he *needed* her...

Brie trembled as she waited for him to unlock the door. She had a feeling he would be rough with her tonight. His eyes shone with dangerous desire.

When he put his hand on the small of her back, she swallowed nervously, letting him lead her inside. This was it. There was no turning back from the ravenous meal he was about to make of her.

He shut the door and dropped his keys on the hall-way table, then commanded as he guided her down the hallway, "Everything off except for the panties. I plan to rip those from your body myself."

He stopped, so she immediately followed his orders and stripped before him, trying to keep the grace of a trained submissive even though she was surprisingly nervous. His sheer maleness overwhelmed her, making it difficult to concentrate.

"Beautiful," he complimented as he pushed her down to her knees so that her mouth was inches from his cock. She knew what he wanted without being asked and unbuckled his belt before unzipping his pants. She eased his throbbing member out of his briefs and opened her mouth to take him.

He grabbed a handful of hair and guided her lips to his cock. "That's it. Suck hard," he snarled lustfully. Brie took the head of his shaft into her mouth and sucked with uninhibited passion, concentrating on the sensitive ridge while her hands worked the base. He groaned in satisfaction, throwing his head back. "Oh, God, those lips…"

She moaned as he forced his cock deeper down into her throat. She wanted to be used in this way, an object for his pleasure. He fucked her mouth without regard for her. Brie relaxed and let him have his way. She was turned on by this selfish need he could not control. She understood it, they both needed the connection and she was thrilled to have the ability to please him.

He finally pulled out, forcing her head back to look at her. "I need to eat you." He helped her to her feet and then pushed her against the wall, ripping her lace thong off her body. With strong arms he grabbed her waist and lifted her up, then putting his hands under her buttocks, he lifted her higher. She squeaked when he commanded that she position her legs over his shoulders. She balanced herself precariously, afraid of being so high—until his tongue found her pussy and she went still. Brie pressed her back against the wall and she found support holding onto his head, all fear gone as he consumed her.

Even his mouth was rough—biting, probing, sucking—but she loved the carnal feel of it. "Yes!" she cried. "Devour me, Master!"

His growl tickled her clit. He returned to his passionate cunnilingus, licking the entire length of her before rimming her ass. She instinctively bucked, taken by surprise by his aggressive tongue.

Brie screamed as she began to tumble forward. With superhuman strength, he caught her and eased her to the floor. "You bad girl… Now your Master must teach you a lesson." He pointed to the center of the living room. "Crawl over there to receive your punishment."

She got on all fours and crawled across the hard marble floor like a cat in heat. She was frightened of her punishment, but desirous of it nonetheless. Once she'd made it to the middle of the room, he commanded gruffly, "Spread your legs wide, and put your left cheek to the floor so you can watch me."

She laid her head against the cool stone, making soft mewing sounds as he approached. He spanked her hard on her right ass-cheek, the sound of it echoing in the room. He slapped her again on the left, and she whimpered. She was sure he had left a handprint that time. He rubbed his hands over both cheeks, bringing a warm caress to complement the tingling sensation he'd created.

He slapped her twice more with the same stinging force, and then he bent down and bit her fiery skin. Brie moaned in ecstasy, the erotic feel of it making her pussy ache.

"Shall we try this again?"

He spread her ass cheeks wide and licked her pussy, starting with her wet opening and traveling all the way up to her anus. Although she gasped when she felt his tongue touch the forbidden area, she did not move. With a hunger she hadn't experienced before, he licked her length the same way several times, like a tiger. The wickedness of it had her mewing in pleasure. He bit her fleshy ass before giving her one more satisfying slap.

He pressed his cock against her pussy without entering as he straddled her thighs, whispering into her ear, "What do you want?"

"I want you to fuck me."

"You want me to fuck you deep enough to hurt?" he

growled hoarsely.

She closed her eyes and voiced her deepest desire. "I want my body to resonate with your thrusts, Master."

He turned her head towards him and kissed her hard, then he held her chin and looked deep into her eyes. It made her shudder, for his gaze reminded her of a ravenous creature's—one that meant her harm.

Part of her yearned for escape. Despite her fear, or because of it, she willingly opened herself to him. "Take me, Master."

He mounted her then, ramming in his cock while holding her waist painfully tight. "I'm going to fuck you like you have never been fucked."

The onslaught began. Brie screamed as he took her violently, just the way she'd asked. Every thrust hit so deep that it sent a wave of painful electricity through her, but it was addictive and she cried out for more.

He was ferocious in his taking of her, fisting her hair and pulling her head back as his powerful hands left bruising caresses. He continually changed angles, seeking to dominate her pussy in ways it had never been conquered.

With each strong thrust, Master was laying his claim. She could feel it approaching, an orgasm like she had never experienced before, born of possession and pain. "Yes, Master, yes!" she cried through grateful tears.

His roar filled the room. "Come for your Master, blossom!"

Brie instantly woke, drenched in sweat, her heart racing as her pussy convulsed in the aftershocks of a powerful orgasm. She reached around desperately in the dark. "Master…? Sir…?"

She found there was no one else in the bed. She lay back down, reality finally sinking in. This was the third night since Sir had left that she had dreamed of Faelan. The intensity of it lingered on her skin like an unwanted caress.

It had seemed so real that she could not free herself from feeling it was an act of betrayal against Sir. Brie hugged herself, tears falling freely down her cheeks. She lay in the bed, trying to rock herself back to sleep, whispering, "No more…"

Trust

Another morning dragged into existence. Even though Brie understood it had only been a dream, the guilt of it weighed heavily on her heart and would not leave her. It cast a dark shadow over her spirit, so much so that she put off going to the Center in hopes of the dreams passing, but she knew she could not waste any more time.

Still feeling out of sorts, Brie headed to the Training Center. She hoped that she might catch Lea while she was there, needing to spend time with her best friend.

When she arrived, Brie went to the front desk and asked for the new headmaster.

The girl smiled pleasantly and asked, "Would you like me to call up Headmaster Coen?"

Brie was surprised the panel had chosen Master Coen rather than Master Anderson to take Sir's place. Although Coen had years of experience working at the Center, from what Brie had observed during her training, Master Anderson had more extensive knowledge and was more affable, as well.

"That would be good, thank you," she answered. Brie stood at the desk waiting for him, her nerves increasing with each passing minute. She had hoped to meet with Master Anderson, who she knew would support the film project. Master Coen? He was an unknown.

The beefy trainer—now headmaster—stepped out of the elevator and walked towards her with his typical stoic face. "Good day, Miss Bennett. What brings you to the Center?"

"My film project, Headmaster Coen. Would it be possible to talk to you about it in private?"

"Certainly. Follow me."

Brie watched his large muscles bulge under his dress shirt. She'd experienced the power of those arms when he'd spanked her...and used a hairbrush. As they took the elevator down to the Training Center itself, she forced herself to break the silence.

"I appreciate you taking the time to talk with me, Headmaster."

"Although I am wading through a mass of paperwork, I have a few minutes I can spare."

She didn't know how to respond so she kept silent, grateful when the elevator doors opened.

As they walked down the hallway to Sir's old office, she was confronted with feelings of déjà vu. Brie closed her eyes for a moment and could almost hear the sounds of Lea and Mary laughing with her in the hallways. It was so strange to think that part of her life was over.

Headmaster Coen opened the door and gestured her inside. Even though the books and pictures on the shelves had changed, it still looked like Sir's office—including the hook attached to the ceiling. She hid her smile.

"What is it you need, Miss Bennett? I have no time for niceties."

"Yes, Headmaster Coen. I have been asked by Mr. Holloway to shoot footage of the school grounds and the equipment used during training."

"I do not have a problem as long as you do not shoot footage of any of our students."

She bowed her head. "Thank you, Headmaster Coen. He also asked that I get interviews with the trainers themselves, and possibly footage of some actual scenes."

When she saw him frown, her heart skipped a beat. So much was riding on his answer. "You may speak to the trainers. If any are willing, you are free to interview them. However, I do not want our training filmed."

She swallowed hard, unsure if simple interviews would be enough for Mr. Holloway.

Headmaster Coen sat back in his chair and sighed. "If—and it is a big if—you can find a trainer and a willing sub on our staff who will consent to being filmed, I give you permission to film one session."

Brie couldn't believe it. Master Coen was giving her exactly what she needed. She stood up and bowed. "Thank you, Headmaster! You don't know how much this will help."

"There is one stipulation, however."

Brie sat back down, afraid that he was about to rip it all away.

"I must approve of any footage you shoot on our

school grounds. I will not interfere with footage you've filmed off the campus, but I insist on having the last word on anything shot here."

"Of course, Headmaster Coen."

"You are free to explore the school and film, provided you do not disturb anyone here."

"I won't, Headmaster Coen." Brie bowed low one last time before leaving. She looked around to make sure no one was watching, and then leapt into the air. She had cleared her first obstacle!

Brie spent the day getting shots of the various rooms that had been used for her practicums, including the first one with the spongy floor and mirrored walls. She remembered vividly that first night when she'd tied the blindfold over her own eyes and presented herself to a complete stranger. That room had been the setting for significant firsts, including her first scene with Faelan when he had been training as a Dom. Visions of her recent dream flashed before her eyes, so she quickly left the room without mentioning the latter experience on film.

Brie moved on to Mr. Gallant's classroom next. Her mind had been opened to the world of submission by the tiny but infinitely wise man. His presence seemed to linger in the classroom even when it was empty.

Brie walked to the bondage room next, the one with the table that she'd first noticed on the website. This room held her most cherished memory—it was where she and Master had begun their physical relationship. She had planned to take a panorama of the room, but decided against it. It was something too personal to share with the rest of the world.

Brie headed down to the auditorium. It was the most significant room in the whole Training Center. This was where she'd been challenged the most. From watching her fellow classmates perform to navigating her own demanding practicums, this was where she'd discovered her power and limits as a submissive. She sat down in one of the chairs and let the memories flood over her.

She was so lost in her private thoughts that she did not hear him behind her until Marquis Gray spoke. "Good afternoon, Miss Bennett."

Brie turned around to see the formidable trainer. His ghostly white skin contrasted against the dark tones of the auditorium. She immediately stood up and bowed out of habit.

"You no longer need to bow, Miss Bennett. I am not your Master."

Brie blushed and looked to the floor, afraid to gaze into his dark, penetrating eyes. "Old habits die hard," she answered.

"Headmaster Coen said you had something to ask me."

Brie felt nervous butterflies start. Being around Marquis was intimidating enough, but when she was trying to conceal something from him, his presence was almost painful. She looked at the camera in her hands, avoiding eye contact at all costs as he sat down beside her.

"I was wonderin—"

"Miss Bennett, look at me."

With apprehension she stared into his dark gaze, holding her breath. She had never been able to hide anything from the experienced trainer.

"You are not doing well," he stated.

She shook her head slightly, afraid she would start to cry if she spoke.

"Gather yourself and explain."

It took a few moments before she could begin. "I have been tormented by dreams, Marquis Gray."

"What kind of dreams, Miss Bennett?"

"Dreams of Faelan."

His expression darkened. "Have you spoken of it to Sir Davis?"

She felt a pit start to grow in her stomach. "No, Marquis Gray."

He shook his head in disappointment. "Describe these dreams to me."

"It has been the same dream the last three nights. It starts right after the collaring ceremony. He takes me to his house as my new Master, and…" She closed her eyes, forcing herself to finish. "We consummate the relationship."

"So in the dream you have chosen Faelan over Sir Davis?"

"Yes," she said meekly.

"How do you feel when you wake up?"

"I feel horrible. It seems so real that I…" she turned away in shame, "…physically respond to them. I feel like I've cheated on Sir."

He was brutally to the point with his question. "Is guilt the reason for your pain, or do you feel regret?"

She protested violently, "No, never regret!" She looked at him in desperation. "Marquis, these dreams are unwanted and yet I am haunted by them when I wake."

He penetrated her with his gaze. She met it bravely, needing him to understand her torment. Finally he spoke. "The dreams are not your responsibility, Miss Bennett. However, your thoughts when you're awake are. Be honest with me—have these dreams changed your feelings towards Mr. Wallace?"

"No! My heart belongs to my Master. Marquis, I cannot live with these feelings of guilt. It's killing me inside. Please help me," she begged.

"I would suggest two things, Miss Bennett. Meditation will help you clear your mind when you awaken, so that this does not affect your waking hours."

She nodded in understanding. "Yes, Marquis. I will do that."

"You must also tell Sir Davis. Be prepared for his displeasure. You should have gone to him first. If you were my sub, I would punish you for such a breach of trust."

Brie felt the pit in her stomach turn into a wave of nausea. What would Sir think of her now?

Marquis replied, "Face the consequences with humility, Miss Bennett, and learn from them. Now, what was it that you needed to ask me?"

Brie ignored the swirling emotions threatening to overtake her and answered the trainer's question about her project. "Marquis Gray, would you be willing to let me interview you about your work here at the Center?"

"Yes, I agree to do a short interview. Mr. Holloway spoke to me of it the other day." His smile was genuine. "I would like to assist you in this."

She was moved by his offer to help. "Thank you, Marquis Gray. Thank you for everything you have done. I know I would not have this opportunity if it weren't for you."

"You are incorrect, Miss Bennett. Your dedication and hard work brought this opportunity, not me."

She would have disagreed, but she knew better than to argue with Marquis Gray. "Then I will simply thank you for your willingness to interview with me."

He nodded curtly. "We will do the interview seven days from now. You may want to check with Mr. Gallant. I believe he's come in early tonight as well."

Brie perked up upon hearing Mr. Gallant's name. She hadn't seen her teacher since graduation. "I will do just that, Marquis Gray."

He raised his eyebrow. "Do not fail to tell Sir Davis about what we discussed."

She blushed with shame and murmured, "I won't. Thank you for your advice."

"You are alumni now, Miss Bennett, but you will forever remain one of my students."

Brie quickly gathered her things, anxious to see Mr. Gallant again and escape from the disgrace lingering in the room. Seeing her teacher would lighten her heavy heart.

She found the small but commanding Dom in his classroom, setting up for the night's class. She was touched when his face broke into a smile the instant he saw her.

"Miss Bennett, what a pleasant surprise."

She held out her hand and he shook it warmly. "How

is the new class, Mr. Gallant?"

"Green and uncertain, but with promising potential."

"Do they remind you of us?"

"No, this group is much more competitive with one another. It will take a bit longer to tame their immaturity."

"May I ask how Candy is doing?"

He looked at her thoughtfully before answering. "That's the girl you recommended, am I correct?"

"Yes, I've been curious how she's faring in class, and if she got rid of the abuser posing as a Dom."

"I cannot speak of her personal life, Miss Bennett. But, as far as her studies are concerned, I am pleased to say she is excelling."

Brie grinned. "I can't tell you how happy that makes me, Mr. Gallant!" She gave him a knowing look. "I'm thrilled someone was willing to sponsor her."

Mr. Gallant didn't blink an eye. "Yes, it is fortunate."

Brie had been told that he was Candy's benefactor, but true to form, Mr. Gallant kept it to himself, not being one to boast.

"In some ways I'm jealous of Candy," she said wistfully, looking around the classroom. "I really enjoyed learning in this room with you."

Concern overshadowed his smile. "Are you satisfied with your new life, Miss Bennett?"

She realized he was picking up on her unease, so she smiled reassuringly. "Yes, Mr. Gallant. I'm overflowing with satisfaction at being collared to Sir."

He seemed appeased by her answer and replied, "That warms my heart to hear."

Brie wanted to hug him, but as a collared submissive she held back the urge. "I came by to ask if you would be willing to do an interview with me for the documentary. I've already gotten permission from Headmaster Coen."

"I am truly sorry, Miss Bennett, but I cannot," he said with regret. "There are family members on my wife's side who would not understand. I will not risk her exposure."

Although Brie was extremely disappointed, she hid it well. "I understand, Mr. Gallant. It sure has been good talking to you again. You made my day, really."

"I miss your enthusiasm, Miss Bennett," he replied. "My wife and I would enjoy having the two of you visit us. After the documentary is complete, of course. I know you have no time to spare these days."

"So true. With Sir off working in New York City and me finishing my project, things are a little crazy right now."

Mr. Gallant frowned. "Sir Davis is away?"

"Yes. But he will be back soon. It's just a week-long business trip."

"I am sorry to hear that, Miss Bennett. It seems regrettable to be separated so early after your collaring."

Brie shrugged her shoulders. "I'm fine, Mr. Gallant. With both of us busy, I can't complain. Please don't concern yourself."

"Very well," he answered, although he did not look convinced. "I need to continue preparing for class. I hope to see you around over the next couple of weeks."

Brie left Mr. Gallant so she could wander the halls of the school, trying to find extra shots, but she soon felt out of place as the Training Center began to fill with people. She looked for Lea but could not find her, so she headed for the elevators to return home.

To her surprise, Ms. Clark was standing before her when the doors opened.

"Miss Bennett."

Brie put her eyes to the floor and mumbled, "Ms. Clark."

The Domme stepped off the elevator and addressed her. "I was told you are doing interviews for your film. Is that right?"

Brie nodded, unsure if she was going to get a lecture about upholding the integrity of the school, a favorite topic of the trainer.

"I will interview with you."

Brie was so shocked, she looked up without thinking. "You will?" When she saw Ms. Clark's stern expression, she instantly looked back down.

"Of course. I believe the perspective of a Domme should be included."

Still recovering from the shock, Brie replied, "I agree."

"Fine. Marquis said you are doing his in exactly a week. I will be available the day after." She did not wait for Brie's response. She walked away, her heels clicking seductively down the hall.

Brie hit the elevator button, still reeling from the shock. The thought of interviewing Ms. Clark made her cringe inside. No doubt Mr. Holloway would approve of the added drama.

The minute she entered the lonely apartment, she dialed Sir's number. Brie dreaded the phone call, but did not hesitate.

Sir could immediately tell something was wrong just by the tone of her 'hello'. "Explain what has happened," he stated, his voice calm and sure. It helped to ease her nerves.

"Sir, I need to tell you that I have had the same dream three nights in a row. It's so real that I..." Her voice trailed off as she lost her courage to continue.

He chuckled, the relief easy to hear in his voice. "You're calling about a dream? Did I die in it? Well, don't worry. I'm fine, babygirl. No need to fret any longer."

"No, Sir... I had a dream about another man."

His tone suddenly became deadly serious. "What man?"

"Faelan, Sir."

He paused before insisting with forced calm, "Explain this dream in detail."

Brie recounted her dream, not leaving out any details, as much as she was desperate to. She would not make the mistake of holding back something he might consider significant, no matter how mortifying it was for her.

The phone went silent. Finally, she asked in a choking gasp. "Sir?"

"How did it make you feel?"

"Every night I wake up feeling I've betrayed you, Sir.

Marquis Gray questioned if my feelings have changed for Faelan, but they have not. These dreams are coming out of nowhere and I just want them to go away."

He said coldly, "Marquis Gray?"

Brie backtracked, realizing she was just digging herself into a deeper hole. "I saw him today at the Center. I didn't want to tell him, Sir, but he insisted. He also was adamant I tell you as soon as I got home."

"Your Master should always be the first you tell," he said in an icy tone. "The fact you have had these dreams for three nights has me questioning your silence."

She blurted, "Sir, I thought they would go away. I thought you would think I was silly or worse, that I actually desired Faelan. Master…after what happened the night before you left, I've been afraid to do or say something wrong."

"So you said nothing."

"Yes," she admitted miserably. "I want to please you, but I also feel a need to protect you, Sir. But in the end, all I ever do is fail you." She stifled a sob, feeling unworthy of his collar.

"Your protection is not what I want from you, Brie. I want your honesty at all times."

She struggled to get the words past the lump in her throat. "Yes, Sir."

"I do not hold you accountable for dreams. You can let go of any feelings of guilt over that. However, I am disappointed."

"I know I deserve to be punished, Sir. Punish me, please."

She heard him sigh heavily. "I'm uncertain if your

dreams are a result of our discussion before I left, but I believe your reluctance to tell me is directly related. It is a vicious cycle. Your fear causes you to be silent, and your secretiveness causes me to question your trustworthiness."

"Yes…" she agreed sadly.

"Brie, anything that causes you discomfort must be shared, no matter the reaction you fear will result from it. Without trust, you and I are nothing."

The truth of his words cut like a knife. "Please punish me."

"I am not without understanding, Brie. As my sub, you need to have faith I will react in a reasonable manner. Our last parting caused you to question that. I give you my word that, even if I need time to digest what you share, I will give you the benefit of the doubt. But only if I hear it from your mouth and *not* another's."

"I promise, Sir. But please, I feel the need to be punished."

"Then your punishment shall be that unfulfilled need."

She whimpered. Brie had never thought in a million years that not being punished could hurt so much.

"Remember this lesson so that we do not have to revisit it again."

After she'd hung up the phone, she let out a painful sigh. This precarious dance of trying to navigate his tragic past—and her foolish missteps—made their relationship difficult and hurtful. Brie could only hope that their love would be enough.

Dangerous Liaisons

B rie knew she could not put off her meeting with Mary any longer. She'd asked Lea to feel out Blonde Nemesis' mental state before she made her first attempt at contact. Lea reported that Mary was willing to get together if it was at a club, not at the Training Center and *not* at Sir's apartment. Brie wondered at the strange request, but remembered Sir's advice to meet Mary on her terms. Before she committed, she called Sir to make sure he approved.

"No, you may not go to The Haven."

Brie was hurt at Sir's lack of trust. "Sir, I don't plan to scene. I will just talk with Mary and Lea and leave afterwards."

He laughed, a response that surprised her. "I am not concerned about you scening, Brie. However, you should know that Mr. Wallace has been given permission to return to the club. I've been informed he is there every night. It would not be appropriate for you to go, especially alone."

Brie wanted to avoid Faelan and all the chaos he

would cause if they were to meet. "Understood, Sir."

"There are several clubs that will do, but they are on the outskirts of the city. See if Mary is open to meeting at one of them instead."

Sir could not know how much his trust in her meant. "Thank you, Sir! I will happily make that suggestion."

"Good luck, Brie. Call me after your meeting."

It turned out that Mary was open to visiting another club, and suggested one that had just reopened. She'd heard it was more edgy than The Haven and wanted to check it out. Neither Lea nor Brie had heard of it, but it was in a central location for them all. Brie picked up Lea in Sir's Lotus. The look on Lea's face when Brie pulled up was priceless.

"Oh my, Brie! Does Sir know you're driving this?"

"Of course. He told me to take his car whenever I want. I'm hoping to impress Mary. Maybe if I let her take a spin she will sign my consent form."

"Do I get to drive it if I sign?" Lea asked.

"Umm…I'll have to ask Sir."

"What?! You trust Mary to drive this hot little sports car more than me?"

"You forget I've seen your poor vehicle. I know the kind of driver you are. How many dents does it have? Fifty?"

"Brie, you're a cruel friend. I'm going to seriously reconsider this whole documentary thing."

"What? And miss out on telling the world your lame jokes as you shake your big boobs? It's an idle threat, girlfriend."

Lea's eyes lit up. "That reminds me, I have a new one."

Brie groaned as she punched the gas pedal and sent both of them slamming into the seats. *Oh, the power of Sir's car!*

"How do you know you have a cheap Dom?"

Brie rolled her eyes. "Just hit me with it."

"He asks you to take off your collar to walk the dog."

Brie actually laughed out loud. "Okay, that was good. You can use that in the interview."

Lea clapped her hands. "I have a good feeling, Brie. I think tonight is going to exceed your wildest dreams."

She sighed nervously. "I hope so. I've never wanted anything as much as this. Well, let me amend that. I have never wanted anything except Sir more than this."

Lea bumped her shoulder and giggled. "Get thee to The Kinky Goat, woman!"

When they arrived a half-hour later and parked, the girls looked at each other and laughed. "This can't be it," Brie stated.

"It says Kinky Goat," Lea replied, pointing to an old, neon sign.

The club was in a rundown section of town and had the vibe of a biker bar. "Is it safe?" Brie asked, reluctant to leave Sir's car unattended.

Lea jumped out of the car. "Where's your sense of adventure, Brie? You've become an old married woman since getting collared. Live a little!"

Brie locked the car and set the alarm. She sincerely hoped she wouldn't regret this…

When they entered the establishment, several of the patrons turned to stare at them. Brie suddenly felt like fresh meat on display and wanted to turn around, but Mary was waving at them from the bar.

"Come on, stick-in-the mud," Lea joked, dragging her over to Mary.

Brie sat down unenthusiastically. She stared at Mary, and Mary stared at her—neither willing to make the first move.

"I have a great joke," Lea started.

Mary broke the silence to avoid it. "How have you been, Stinky Cheese?"

Brie answered half-heartedly, "Good, and you?"

"Could be better. Could be a hell of a lot better."

Brie didn't want to pussyfoot around the elephant in the room. "Why did you do it? Why did you let me think you fucked Faelan at the graduation ceremony? Why on earth would you do that to a friend?"

"It's always about you, isn't it, Brie? Did it ever occur to you that I had feelings for Faelan?"

"What? Like you did for every guy I showed an interest in?"

"See! There you go again. You think I liked those men because you did? Hell, no! You and I have the same tastes, but for some damn reason they always go for you," Mary spat out angrily, then took a drink of her rum and Coke.

"Are you seriously telling me that you love Faelan?"

"Love is too strong a word, and something you throw around like candy. I want him on a level I have never wanted another man. You'd probably call that love, but that would be stupid."

Brie snorted. "Oh, yeah. Call me stupid, but at least I'm honest about my feelings. You just push everyone away."

Mary waved her hand and ordered a round of drinks for the three of them. "You are such a bitch, Brie. You think you're all goodness and light, but you are a bitch underneath. Guys are idiots and fall for bitches like you all the time."

Lea spoke up. "Look, Mary, don't take out your frustrations on Brie. She cares for people and that's something you wish you had, even if you hate her for it."

Mary stood up and looked like she was going to throw her drink in Lea's face, but Brie put her hand firmly on Mary's wrist.

"Maybe I *am* a bitch, because you're right—you and I are a lot alike, and you are the biggest bitch I know."

Mary looked at her in shock and then started laughing. Brie joined in and soon all three girls filled the bar with their laughter.

A sleazy wannabe Dom eased up to them. "You do realize laughing is not allowed. Sit down and shut your mouths and I may treat you to my whip."

His uncouth approach was comical. Brie looked at Lea and then Mary. The three burst out in giggles, embarrassing the 'Dom' enough that he left.

"Oh, my God, I've missed this!" Lea stated.

Mary sat down and sipped her drink before admitting, "Me too."

Brie grinned at the two girls. "I've felt lost without my other Musketeers." She gave Mary a humorous snarl. "I just couldn't get past you betraying me like that."

"I was honest for the first time in my life and look what happened. The guy tossed me away like garbage and my friends turned on me."

Brie suddenly felt the weight of her rejection and grabbed Mary's hand, squeezing it tightly. "You're right. I sucked as a friend because I never considered you were telling the truth. Well...that's not quite true. When I went to present my collar I saw the look on your face. It helped me to have the courage to present it to Sir instead."

"You should be bowing at my feet, thanking me," Mary answered.

Brie took a sip of her drink as a peace offering, even though she didn't care for rum and Coke. "Yeah, that'll happen..."

Lea held up her drink. "Here's to the Three Musketeers reuniting!" The three clinked glasses. Brie noticed the sleazy wannabe Dom raised his glass too. It was pathetic, so she turned her back on him.

"Lea said something about the documentary," Mary started. "Don't you dare tell me you need me to spill my guts on film."

Brie took a gulp of the drink for liquid courage and smiled, throwing all caution to the wind. "That's exactly what I need. I showed the piece to a big-time producer and you know what he had the nerve to tell me? And I quote: 'You don't have a film unless you get Mary's story'."

Mary smiled. "Hah!"

"I'm completely serious."

Mary got a superior look on her face. "So the great Brie Bennett came here tonight with her tail tucked between her legs to beg for my story."

Brie replied dryly, "There will be no begging, bitch."

Mary bristled at her tone and was about to let Brie have it when Lea stepped in. "Hey, Virginal Mary, I thought this was a club but all I see is the lame-o bar."

Mary turned to her. "You're an idiot, Lea. The action takes place in the back." She pointed to the double doors across the room. "I'm told all kinds of fun happens behind those doors."

"Yeah, like it could even compare to The Haven," Brie retorted.

Lea rubbed her hands together gleefully. "Why don't we check it out and see for ourselves?"

Brie knew Lea was attempting to defuse Mary's anger, so she went along with it. "Why not?"

Mary looked at her scornfully. "I'm shocked the collared Brie would consent to having fun. Won't your Master get mad and punish you?"

"I'm not going to scene, you ignoramus. I'm just curious."

"Well, hell, so am I!" Lea answered, getting up. "Let's go…"

Brie followed the other two into the Play Arena. She was shocked at how rundown and grimy the place was. She looked around, not impressed by the old equipment. Everything about it felt icky and slimy.

She glanced over at a girl bent over a table. The blindfolded sub had a ball gag in her mouth and was dripping saliva profusely. Her hands were tied behind her back, and her legs were spread and bound so that her pussy was splayed out for all to see. Written on her ass were the words, 'Fuck Doll'.

Brie looked away when a random guy dropped his pants and warned the girl that he played rough and was going to make it hurt.

She quickly moved on to another scene with a Domme and two subs. The male sub was dressed in a black leather hood and matching collar. His cock was restrained by a painful-looking metal gadget that fastened around both his balls and the head of his cock, making the shaft bend in an unnatural manner. He was standing over the female sub, who was lying on a rickety bench. She was licking his balls enthusiastically while the Domme fucked her with a lengthy black dildo strapped on at the hips. The Domme's strokes were long and ruthless.

"Now, thumperboy, you better not get any harder or it's going to hurt." She slapped the female. "Suckle those balls, slut. Make it hard for him." She laughed wickedly as she spread the girl's outer lips and thrust even deeper.

Somewhere in the back, Brie could hear a girl whimpering as a whip cracked repeatedly. "Shut your piehole, cunt, or I'll make it really hurt."

Overall, the place lacked the cleanliness and allure of The Haven, so Brie opted out. "I'll meet you back at the bar. Don't take too long, you two," she warned.

Brie sat at the bar, feeling on edge. She took a sip of

her drink and snarled. Leave it to Mary to order her a crappy drink. After several minutes, Brie started drinking it out of sheer boredom. Even though she didn't enjoy the taste, at least it gave her something to do.

She waited impatiently, getting more agitated by the minute. That was when the sleazy wannabe Dom came over to make his move. "I see your girlfriends have decided to have a little fun. Why don't you and I join them?"

Brie shook her head, and was surprised to feel a little lightheaded. "Look, I'm collared." She touched the beloved collar around her neck for emphasis. "I don't scene with anyone except my Master. It's rude of you to even ask."

The guy didn't seem to care and sat down beside her. "We're both grown adults here. What we do doesn't have to leave this place. It's just you and me enjoying a little time together." He reached over and stroked her arm.

Brie pulled away, but her reflexes were unusually sluggish. "Don't…"

He smiled. "Don't what? Don't flirt with the sexiest girl at the bar?"

Her limbs began to feel heavy and weak. She looked at her hands, wondering what was wrong. But then she remembered the sleaze sitting next to her and barked, "Go."

He ignored her demand, opening his mouth to show off the stud in his tongue. "I'm going to make you come."

Brie giggled at the ludicrous thought.

He grinned at her lustfully, taking her response as consent. "I'm going to ram your ass with a dildo while I eat your cunt."

She let out a snorting giggle, as if she were drunk. Brie looked at her drink, but it was still half full. She couldn't explain why she thought he was so funny.

"After you come, I'll tie you up and make you pay for laughing at me earlier."

She broke out in a peal of laughter as she watched the room begin to move of its own accord.

"I think you would make the perfect fuck doll, princess. Don't you?" he said as he grabbed her arm.

Despite her confusion, Brie's internal alarms sounded loudly and she struggled against his firm grasp. "No…"

"No means yes and yes means no," he replied with a sly grin.

She had to think for a few seconds to answer him. "Yes."

He grunted in triumph. "I knew you wanted it. Come with me." He pulled her off the chair.

She struggled against him, but she could barely stand and fell into his arms. "That's it, come with Daddy," he encouraged, guiding her towards the double doors. "Daddy's going to have all kinds of fun with you tonight."

Brie no longer resisted, desperate for his support when the floor began to wobble beneath her feet.

"Let her go," a deep voice demanded from behind her.

"Stay out of this," the sleaze answered.

"I'm serious. I will count to three. Let her go or you will leave with a mouthful of broken teeth."

The sleaze held onto Brie tighter. "This one's mine."

"One…two…"

Brie suddenly felt herself falling. Solid arms caught her and lifted her up.

"You're safe, kitten."

Brie focused on his hazel eyes just before everything began to spin.

She woke up feeling groggy and was surprised to find herself lying on a couch. *This isn't Sir's apartment!* The place had the feel of a bachelor pad, with its minimal décor and large entertainment system.

Brie began to hyperventilate, remembering the sleaze who had been holding her just before she'd passed out. A number of scenarios went through her head, each one more terrible than the last. A sob escaped her lips.

"You're awake."

Brie knew that voice and turned towards it in relief. "Baron…"

He got up from his chair and walked over to her. "What the hell were you thinking, kitten?"

"How?" she asked, so woozy she was unable to form sentences.

"How did you get here? I found you being dragged off to have sex with a lowlife. What were you thinking going to a place like that?"

All she could manage was, "Lea? Mary?"

"They're fine. I sent them home and brought you here to recover. There must have been something in your drink. Probably that bastard, but no one saw him do it and I couldn't get him to admit to it, despite my powers of persuasion. So I decided to give him a personal warning just in case. He won't be fucking a girl anytime soon."

Brie shuddered, realizing how close she'd come to being raped.

"Why...you?"

"Why was I there? I heard it'd reopened and went to look after newbies who might wander into the place. That club is bad news. I never thought I would find one of our graduates there, much less three of them."

Brie buried her head into the couch. "Sir?"

"Yes, I called him to let him know what's happened. He's on a plane flying back as we speak."

Brie began to cry. Baron lifted her up off the couch and embraced her.

"You're safe. Nothing happened."

She sobbed, soaking Baron's large shoulder with her tears. Finally, she choked out a weak, "Thank you."

He held her tightly. "You're okay, kitten. Nobody hurt you."

She gulped through her tears, "You...are...a good...man."

His warm chuckle rumbled in his chest. "No. I simply cannot abide women being abused."

"Baron..." she gasped, still struggling to think straight.

He crushed her in his safe embrace. "Don't speak, kitten. Sit here while I make you something to eat." Baron put her down and repositioned the pillow so she could sit up. He returned a short time later with a bowl of oatmeal and some hot tea.

"Drink," he commanded, bringing the cup up to her lips.

Brie opened her mouth and the warm liquid brought its soothing relief, caressing her throat. He put the cup down and lifted a spoonful of the hot cereal to her lips.

"You'll feel better soon."

"Thank you," she said. A tear fell down her cheek.

He wiped it away. "No need to cry."

Baron gave her another spoonful. She looked around his apartment, noting several photos of a beautiful woman with dark skin, an inviting smile and a collar around her neck.

"Your submissive, Baron?" she asked, pointing to a photo.

He looked at the photo and nodded slowly. In a quiet voice he added, "We're parted."

Brie frowned, sad to learn that Baron was alone.

"Eat," he insisted, letting her know it was not a topic up for discussion.

After the bowl was empty and the last sip of tea had been drunk, he tucked the blanket around her and ordered her to sleep. She settled down, not thinking sleep was possible.

"Brie…"

She felt a gentle nudge and heard her name again. *Master's voice.*

Her eyes flew open and she saw Sir's beloved face. He sat beside her and pulled her onto his lap, rocking her as if she were a child. She buried her face in his chest and cried with relief.

"Shhh, babygirl. I'm here now…"

Lovers to Friends

The fallout from the incident affected Brie in ways she could not have imagined. Sir was angry with himself. "Here I was so concerned about Wallace that you ended up going to a *den* of wolves. Well, that won't happen again, Brie," he stated forcibly.

Brie worried about what it would mean for her—for them both. Sir seethed with a quiet anger she could not reach past. She was grateful when he finally decided to speak with his friend Master Anderson. After several visits with him, Sir set up a long meeting with Marquis Gray.

She had no idea what had been discussed, but when Sir returned from Marquis Gray he seemed more like himself. "Sit with me, Brie."

She moved over to him and sat on the couch. "Yes, Sir?"

"I realize I have not been easy to live with lately, and you have suffered for it."

"It has been difficult, Sir," she admitted, bowing her head.

"Brie, unfortunately you are collared to a man haunted by ghosts of the past. I have been shaped by those events and cannot react the way most people do."

"I accept that, Sir."

He swept her hair back gently. "You are a challenge for me in so many ways, téa." She looked at him questioningly. In response, Sir pressed her head against his chest and held her tightly against him. "I couldn't save my father, but I damn well am going to protect you."

She smiled, content in her Master's caring embrace.

They spent the afternoon unpacking the rest of her boxes, making her stay more permanent for them both. During their work, Sir came across the wax casting Tono had made of her. He held it up and stared at it for a while before announcing, "I believe I will call Tono and ask if he can come over tonight. The meeting has been put off for far too long."

"If it pleases you, Sir," she answered. Brie wondered how she would feel when she saw Tono. So much had happened since graduation—it seemed like a lifetime ago.

When the doorbell rang later that evening, Brie felt only peace as she opened the door to her former training Dom. Tono's eyes were as gentle and kind as she remembered, despite the reality of their past. He handed her a bottle of sake.

"It is good to see you, Miss Bennett."

It was strange hearing him call her 'Miss Bennett' and not 'Toriko'. She took the bottle graciously. "Thank you, Tono Nosaka." She gestured him inside, then closed the door slowly behind him, struck by how surreal it was to invite Tono into Sir's apartment.

"Thank you for coming, Ren," Sir said, getting up from the couch. He shook Tono's hand and then instructed Brie, "Set the sake in the kitchen and start a pot of water boiling."

Brie bowed and followed his orders, assuming the boiling water must be the way to warm sake. When she returned to Sir, she was surprised to see his hand on Tono's shoulder and a serious look on his face. Tono nodded once and turned to Brie.

"You are completing your documentary. It pleases me to hear it."

She avoided his gaze, suddenly feeling uncomfortable. The last time they'd talked, he'd told her how proud he was of her work and that he would support Brie's career as her Dom. Guilt clouded her heart, making it painfully clear that she was *not* ready for this meeting.

Sir answered for her. "Yes, Brie is working diligently on it. Mr. Holloway has some suggestions she is currently filming. Why don't we move to the kitchen and Brie can tell you about it?"

Tono and Brie sat at the table while Sir took out a small flask. Brie couldn't bring herself to speak, so she watched as Sir poured the sake into the flask before placing it in the boiling water.

"What were you asked to add?" Tono inquired.

Brie blushed and turned to him, smiling hesitantly. "Shots of the Training Center, interviews with trainers, and…more in-depth interviews with Lea and Mary."

Sir interjected, "That is how the three inadvertently ended up at the club."

Tono nodded in understanding.

Brie felt heat rise to her cheeks, knowing that Tono had been informed of the incident at The Kinky Goat. She looked away, feeling the shame of the experience wash over her.

She felt Sir's hand on her shoulder. "But that is not why I asked you to come tonight." Sir set three sake cups on the table and poured the warmed sake into them before sitting down. "How is your family, Ren?"

"My father returned to Japan last week. My family in general is in good health."

"To your family's continued good health," Sir stated, holding up a small sake cup.

He handed Brie her sake, and she held it up before sipping the warm rice wine. It had a plum flavor that was slightly sweet and incredibly tasty.

She stared at the cup, trying to build up the courage to ask, "Was your father relieved when I did not choose you?"

Tono waited until she looked up and met his unwavering gaze. "He feels you made the appropriate choice, Miss Bennett."

Brie looked back down at her cup, unsure how to respond.

"Ren, it is fine to call her Brie. 'Miss Bennett' is too formal given your history together."

Tono picked up his cup and nodded. "To both of you."

"I'll drink to that," Sir answered.

Brie lifted her cup and swallowed the last of the sake in it. Sir immediately filled up Tono's and Brie's cups and announced, "I'm heading off to the spare room to unpack Brie's remaining boxes. I want to give you two a chance to speak freely."

An uncomfortable silence filled the room when Sir left. It was broken when Tono said, "Brie, I understand your choice."

She looked at him sadly.

He shook his head. "No, I do not need or want your sympathy. You made your choice. I accept it."

When Brie did not answer, Tono leaned forward. "Your guilt does not honor me or what we shared." He sat back in his chair slowly. "Seeing you happy is my only consolation at this point."

"I…I never meant to hurt you."

"Someone was going to get hurt. I knew what was at stake going in. I do not regret our time together, Brie. Do you?"

"No, Tono Nosaka, I do not."

"Then we both move on, better for the time we shared together."

"Yes," she agreed.

They both drank their sake and he poured another round before stating, "I am looking into working with couples new to Kinbaku. There are many who would like to learn the art."

"I'm sure there are, and you would be the perfect man to teach them. You have a patient soul and a true talent."

"I'm currently looking for a sub to join me for the beginner courses. Most only want to be involved if there are advanced rope techniques or suspension involved."

"That's a shame. Even your simplest work is inspiring."

He laughed good-naturedly. "Yes, I remember how easily you gave in to the rope."

She joined in his laughter. "I think a lot of that had to do with your 'breathe with me' technique."

"I will not deny there is method to my madness."

She dared to look the handsome Japanese Dom in the eye. "I think you are an exceptional person, Tono Nosaka."

His expression softened. "I feel the same, Brie. So this is where we go from lovers to friends."

She picked up her cup. "To you, my friend."

"To us."

Tono shared some of his recent foibles in scening, including one with a new sub. The girl had had a panic attack while he had been hoisting her up, but her reaction had been to giggle hysterically. Everyone watching had thought she was having a wonderful experience, but he'd noticed her rapid breathing. He had asked her if she had reached red, but she'd shaken her head and giggled louder.

After several minutes, he had decided something wasn't right and had cut her down. She'd grabbed onto him, laughing all the way to a private room. The entire club had laughed along with her even as they'd abandoned the scene.

"When I asked her why she'd answered no to being red, she told me she'd heard, 'Do you eat sweetbread?'"

Tono had Brie laughing so hard that Sir came out to investigate.

"What is going on here?"

Brie was pointing at Tono, snickering. "Sweetbread!"

Tono shrugged. "She's easily amused."

Sir nodded in agreement. "Yes, it doesn't take much." He looked at her and smiled—the first relaxed smile since his return.

With the pleasant buzz of the sake flowing through her veins, she momentarily forgot Tono was there and purred, "I love you, Sir."

He walked over and kissed the top of her head. "I try to convince myself that being easily amused is not the reason you chose me."

She broke out in another peal of laughter that both Doms joined in on. The night ended on that light note.

Sir asked Brie to see Tono out while he stayed in the kitchen to wash up. She walked Tono to the door and smiled when he held out his hand to her.

"Good night, Brie. It's been a pleasure."

She took it, grateful they no longer had that awkward barrier between them. "Likewise, Tono Nosaka."

After shutting the door, she returned to Sir to thank him, but the amorous look in his eyes told her he had other things on his mind.

"Come to me, téa."

She glided over to her Master's wet hands, and squealed when Sir swept her off her feet. He started towards the bedroom, pronouncing, "I'm going to fuck your sweetbreads."

Brie giggled all the way down the hall.

The Solution

Sir insisted that Brie meet with Mary and Lea again, but this time in the safe confines of the Training Center. "I will spend time with Master Coen while you three speak. There are several issues he and I need to go over, now that he has taken over as headmaster."

Brie was curious, knowing that Sir had recommended Master Anderson take over the position when he'd resigned, so she asked, "Sir, how do you feel about the panel's choice?"

"I made my recommendation. However, I am confident Coen will make a fine headmaster."

"What will Master Anderson do now?" Brie hated the thought of future subs missing out on the experienced Dom's unique skills.

"He is taking over Coen's training position, but has not committed to staying longer until he sees how this new session plays out."

"I hope he stays, Sir."

He looked down at her with a smirk. "Want to feel the bite of his bullwhip again, téa?"

Brie shook her head. "Not for that reason, Master. I want him to stay because he's your friend."

Sir surprised her by giving her a peck on the cheek. "You are a sweet little thing."

Sir treated Brie to a spirited drive to the Training Center in his Lotus. The sports car was like an extension of his body and he knew precisely how to use and abuse it for his enjoyment. He kept Brie's heart pounding the entire way, helping to temporarily relieve her of the anxiety she felt about meeting Mary again.

She walked into the college, laughing as she hung onto Sir's arm. Business students standing at the entrance turned to see what the commotion was about. Brie buried her face in Sir's arm. "Sorry, Sir." She knew as a submissive she was not supposed to bring attention to herself.

He chuckled, patting her hand. "It's all right, Brie. The students here are far too serious. They could do with a little laughter."

Sir took her to the lower level and walked her to the meeting room where Lea and Mary were waiting. He handed Brie her briefcase and nodded to the two women. "Good afternoon, Ms. Taylor, Miss Wilson."

They both greeted Sir, but Brie was surprised to hear a hint of repentance in Mary's voice.

Sir nodded to them both and turned back to Brie. "I will be meeting with Headmaster Coen in his office. Go there when you are finished."

"Yes, Sir," Brie said, bowing gratefully. Whatever happened today, Sir would be there to support and encourage her. She watched him walk down the hall before she entered the room.

Lea ran to her, then hugged her tightly. "Oh, Brie, I'm so sorry about what happened. Are you okay?"

"I'm fine. Baron stopped the creep before anything happened."

"But it must have been frightening, knowing what almost... And we were right there," Lea said with tears in her eyes.

Mary snarled, "As soon as he brought you into the Play Arena, I would have been all over his ass. No way would I have let him touch you! What, did he think we wouldn't notice or wouldn't care?" Brie could tell Mary was boiling with pent-up rage.

Brie walked over to her and put her arm around Mary's shoulders. "I know you would have protected me."

Mary's voice was rough with emotion. "I never meant for that to happen, Brie. I know you blame me—everyone does."

Brie squeezed her shoulder in reassurance. "No. I don't, and I know Sir doesn't. I should have trusted my gut when I saw how rundown it was, but like you, I was curious."

Mary pulled away, but slowly, as if she wanted the contact but felt uncomfortable with it.

Brie turned to Lea. "So let's sit down and talk about the documentary. It's the whole reason we got into that mess in the first place."

"I'm in—whatever you want, however you want it," Lea said, sitting down beside her.

"No," Brie said. "Hear me out before you agree to anything."

Lea propped her chin up with both hands. "Okay, shoot!"

"Mr. Holloway wants your honest stories. He won't settle for superficial crap. But if you do this, you will become an easy target for the haters out there. It could get really ugly." She looked sympathetically at Lea. "And you'd have to tell your mom everything. Is that something you're willing to face?"

"Obviously you are," Lea stated. "If you're willing to jump into the lions' den, I'll jump with you."

Both Brie and Lea stared at Mary.

"What the hell? I don't even know why you're asking. I told you from the beginning I wasn't going to get all personal. Did you really think I would change my mind?"

Brie suddenly had an idea, realizing exactly how to sway her. "I remember a story you once told me. One about a little girl who watched *It's a Wonderful Life* and decided to become a pharmacist so she could save lives. Well, I think you could save lives with this film. From the abuse you suffered and *survived*, to learning the importance of full disclosure in a scene, the mistakes you and I made could prevent others from suffering the same consequences—or worse. I plan to include what happened to me at The Kinky Goat," she added with seething rage, "because I don't want any girl to fall victim to a creep like that." She wiped away the angry tears that fell from her eyes. "Mary, everything we've learned—all of it—will be lost if you don't agree to do this."

Mary just glared at her, saying nothing.

Brie leaned forward and said with confidence, "I know you aren't a coward."

Mary responded by growling and pushing away from the table. Brie simply sat there and stared at her, letting it sink in.

"No means no!" Mary hollered, getting up from the table. She paced around the room furiously, muttering to herself.

Lea gave Brie a cautious thumbs-up.

Finally, Mary sat back down. "I know I will regret this and hate you for the rest of my life."

Brie opened her briefcase and pulled out the consent forms. "Now, there's no need to sign this today. Read it over; make sure you understand everything before you sign, anyway."

Mary grabbed it from her and signed it immediately.

"What are you doing?" Brie cried.

"I know myself. If I take this home I'll tear it into a million pieces." She glared at the form and then shoved it in Brie's face. "Better take it from me now."

Brie quickly placed it back in the briefcase and shut the lid. "I don't think you're going to regr—"

"Shut up, Brie. Just shut up," Mary snarled.

Brie knew better than to push her any further. A nervous happiness started to build inside. It was really happening… Mary, her Nemesis, her frienemy, had agreed.

"So do you guys want to see what I already have?"

Mary shrugged, but Lea clapped her hands. "Damn tootin', I wanna see how I look in this film." She asked with a grin, "Does it make my boobs look bigger?" Lea adjusted her breasts with her hands for dramatic emphasis.

"Naturally," Brie answered, pulling out her laptop as the other two gathered around. "Now, feel free to tell me what doesn't work for you. I'll be filming a lot of new shots, so I have plenty of room to play."

They spent the next hour and a half laughing their way through six weeks of training. Brie kept sneaking glances at the other two, overflowing with happiness. This journey they were on had not ended at the Center like she'd thought—it was truly just beginning.

Brie walked to Sir's old office, listening to the sexy echo of her heels in the hallway. Surprisingly, one of the most useful things she'd learned was how to walk in six-inch heels. It had given her a seductive power she'd never had before, and she basked in the glory of it as she swayed her hips.

She knocked on the office door. Even though she knew Master Coen was headmaster now, it surprised her to hear his voice order from within, "Enter."

Brie opened the door and had to catch her breath. Sir was holding a thin iron rod in his hands. She took a step back and then dropped her gaze to the floor. *The brand!*

"Well, it appears it's time for you to go," Headmaster Coen told Sir. "Thank you for your time."

She sneaked a peek and saw Sir put the brand in a thin wooden box, before shaking Coen's hand. "My pleasure, and thank you for this," he added, holding up the box.

Brie shuddered.

Sir winked at Brie as he walked her out. "How did it go, Brie?"

She immediately forgot about the brand and grabbed onto his arm. "Sir, Mary said yes!"

"Excellent."

"You were right. My assumptions about Mary were way off."

He looked at her compassionately. "I have found that is normally the case, Brie. What we think to be true has nothing to do with reality."

She pressed closer to him. "You're so wise, Master."

"You have called me 'wise' once before. Did I not tell you that I prefer intelligent, quick-witted or experienced?"

She giggled, remembering their conversation at the club after Master Anderson's bullwhip session. "Yes, Sir. I do recall you saying that a *long* time ago. Can you forgive your wayward sub for forgetting?"

He slapped her on the ass. "I should take you home for a thorough spanking, so that it will remain fresh in your mind."

She wiggled her butt suggestively. "If it pleases you, Sir."

When they arrived home, he handed her the dark wooden box to carry up to the apartment. He was not letting her forget that it existed. She stood in the mirrored elevator, staring ahead, her body tingling with fear. She noticed that Sir looked completely relaxed and unconcerned, as if this was an everyday happening. Would he try to brand her tonight?

Will I let him?

Brie looked down at the box with tears pricking her eyes. The fear evoked by Master Coen's 'mock branding' still resonated in her mind. Sir was asking too much...

As devoted as she was to Sir, Brie did not want to endure the pain of the brand—even if it would please him.

When they entered the apartment, Sir sat down on the couch and asked her to kneel at his feet. "Give me the box, téa."

Brie held it up with shaking hands.

He opened the wooden box reverently and smiled. He picked up the simple iron rod with a handle on one end and a 'T' on the other, and twirled it between his fingers. "There are two things I am quite aware of, téa. You are not a masochist, and you are afraid of this brand."

He looked down at her. Brie nodded in agreement, not trusting herself to speak.

"You will not wear my brand until you beg for it. Until that time, it will remain in this box, unused." He gave her a benevolent look, adding, "I promise—even if it means you never ask." He placed it back in the box and closed the lid, latching it. "Put it on the top shelf of our closet."

She rocked back to her feet and walked down the hallway without speaking, grateful he was not forcing it on her. She pushed the wooden box far into the back of the closet, with no desire to feel its skin-melting touch. However, knowing that Sir wanted her to wear his brand was powerful. Even more potent was the knowledge that he was leaving it up to her.

She walked back to him and settled at Sir's feet once more, purring silently as he ran his fingers through her hair.

"I know this will not come as welcome news, téa, but my clients are returning to Russia and have requested I join them. The purpose of my visit is to observe their factory practices, so that their managers can be properly trained for the relocation."

Brie looked up at him, unable to hide her disappointment.

"This will be at least a three-week trip."

She opened her mouth to protest, but thought better of it.

"But I am not leaving you alone again. Completing your film is paramount and you need support for that. Normally, I would suggest you stay with a friend, but given recent events, I am not comfortable with that option. After much thought and soul-searching, I have come up with a solution I think will serve both our needs."

"I don't understand, Master." Brie shook her head, an icy chill running down her spine. "I have a feeling I don't want to understand."

He lifted her chin, forcing Brie to focus on him and not on her growing concern. "Your safety and well-being are the only things that matter to me. Since you cannot come with me, I will leave you here in the hands of another."

Her heart skipped a beat. "Master?"

"I will give him full rights as your Master, bar one."

"Rights?" she cried out in alarm.

"In every way you will serve as his submissive. However, he will not have the right of penetration. I expect you to obey every command without question or suffer his punishment when you fail. I have instructed him not to be lenient with you."

"No…" The weight of Sir's abandonment crushed Brie's heart like a heavy stone.

"Téa, this is my command. I cannot stay and I will not leave you alone. You must obey me in this."

"Please, Master, don't ask this of me."

"I am not asking," he replied.

She bowed her head, struggling between shock and grief.

"Look at me, téa." Brie forced herself to look into her Master's eyes, unable to hide her feelings of resentment. He said with gruff emotion, "I have promised to protect you. I can do no less."

"But…giving me to another? Don't you love me?" she whimpered.

"It is the force that drives me. You need to be supported, not only as a submissive, but in your film endeavors." He caressed her cheek tenderly, his gaze certain and kind. "My love for you is without question, Brie."

She jumped when the doorbell rang.

He nodded. "Answer it."

Brie fought with her conflicting emotions. She did not have to answer the door. Sir could not force her to give herself to another Master. If push came to shove, she had the option to leave...

"Obey me," he commanded with gentle firmness.

Looking into his eyes again, she saw only love for her. Sir was not asking her to do this for himself. This was a sacrifice of love on his part.

She got up and walked to the door, her heart pounding as she reached for the doorknob. Which trainer would it be? Marquis? He was a disciplinarian and had an interest in helping her with the film. Or would it be Master Anderson, the bullwhip master who was also Sir's good friend? Either would be a challenge she wasn't sure she was ready for.

Brie took a deep breath and opened the door.

His soothing gaze washed over her like a wave in the ocean.

"Toriko..."

The Contract

B rie stood holding the door open, staring at Tono in shock.

"Invite him in, téa."

She shook her head slightly to regain her bearings before bowing to the Dom. "Please come in, Tono Nosaka." She stepped aside to allow him to pass, not daring to look in his direction.

In a daze, Brie closed the door and walked back to Sir, then knelt at his feet—her place of comfort. Tono sat at the other end of the couch, beside Sir.

Sir began petting her hair lightly. "She just became aware of the arrangement."

"Her thoughts?" Tono asked.

"I do not know." Sir lifted Brie's chin. "What do you think, téa?"

Her lips trembled when she spoke. "If I am to serve another, then Tono is a fine choice, Sir."

Sir glanced over at Tono. "She is still struggling with my decision."

Tono addressed Brie. "Do you wish to serve me, toriko? I will not allow you to serve under me unless it is your desire."

Brie dropped her eyes to stare at the floor. "I do not understand what this arrangement entails, Tono Nosaka. I cannot answer you."

"Spoken like an intelligent woman," Sir commented, kissing the top of her head. "I will keep you in suspense no longer. Ren and I still have to iron out the details. Come join us at the table. I want you to be fully aware of what I am asking of both of you."

Sir stood up and went to his desk to retrieve a file. "I had this drawn up. Naturally, it is subject to change, depending on our discussion tonight."

Tono followed him to the kitchen table, with Brie several feet behind both men. Her head was buzzing like a hornet's nest with thoughts…and fears.

Sir indicated that Tono should sit opposite him, but he pulled the other chair close to himself and commanded gently, "Sit."

Brie sat down robotically, and kept her eyes glued to her lap. *This isn't really happening…*

Her Master pushed the folder across the table towards Tono. "Read over the contract. Anything you do not agree with or need clarification on, I want to address now. This is as much for téa's benefit as for yours."

Brie heard Tono turn the pages slowly as he read over the contract. When he was done, he asked, "Do you have a pen?"

"Of course," Sir answered. "Téa?"

Brie obediently stood up and retrieved a pen from the desk. She returned to Sir, but he nodded towards

Tono. She held it out with an open hand, her insides quivering when he made physical contact. "Thank you, toriko."

Such simple words, yet everything had changed with Sir's decision. This man would soon be her Master—if she allowed it.

"It states the duration of this contract begins tomorrow and ends exactly three weeks from that date?"

"Actually, that should be amended to 'or upon my return'. Should I arrive earlier, I would expect to regain my rights as her Master and should I need to stay longer, I would want téa to remain in your care and under your protection."

"Understood." Tono scribbled something in the margin and continued, "I see that I am not allowed to 'lend' her to another, but I want to clarify that you have no objection to her being part of a demonstration. Although she will be working on the documentary, I plan to have her assist me in a weekly class. Will that be a problem?"

"As long as completing the film is your top priority, I do not have an issue with her participating in a class. However, you must be the one in charge of téa. No one else touches her," Sir stated emphatically.

"Even to recreate a knot?"

Sir sighed and closed his eyes, rubbing his temples. "Simple guided instruction is fine. However, I do not want her to scene with one of your inexperienced Doms."

"I would never put Brie in that situation," Tono assured him. Brie noted that he wrote the words '*guided instruction only'* in the margin.

"I see I am not allowed to take her from the city limits."

"No."

"Because my classes take place at The Haven, I see no conflict."

"Ah, but The Haven may be an issue. I do not want Brie running into Wallace there."

Tono nodded in agreement. "We shall enter from the back and proceed to the training room. We will in no way provoke an encounter. However, if he seeks us out, it will be dealt with."

"I do not trust the boy—yet. Although Marquis is working with Wallace, I still consider him a threat to himself and Brie."

Brie was surprised to hear that Faelan was being personally instructed by Marquis. She wondered if it had anything to do with her talk with the trainer.

"Acceptable," Tono replied, looking farther down the contract. "I will need further explanation of the 'no penetration' clause."

"It is simple enough. There is to be no penetration of her anally, vaginally, or orally with any tool or body part."

"Does that include kissing?"

Sir stared at Brie's lips for several moments before answering. His voice was gruff and low as he replied grudgingly, "I will allow kissing."

Tono took the pen and clearly wrote, *'kissing excluded'*.

Brie blushed. It was strange to have these two men discussing such things. She looked to the floor, her heart beating erratically.

"It states I am in charge of her care, protection and well-being. Are there any specific needs you require me to meet?"

"Naturally, her documentary comes above everything else. I expect you to give her the time and environment necessary for her to succeed in meeting her deadline. I am not opposed to having her performing necessary tasks for you, as long as it does not jeopardize the project."

"You and I are agreed on that."

Sir snorted. "Just as important to me, I expect you to keep her safe, Ren. No run-ins with Mr. Wallace, no unescorted clubbing while I am gone... Keep her safe."

"I assure you, she will be looked after."

"After what occurred during my last trip..." Sir shook his head angrily. "I cannot be reasonable on that score."

Brie glanced at Sir, noticing his clenched jaw and the throbbing vein in his neck. As much as this action seemed extreme, she understood the motive behind it. It was his need to protect her that had inspired the unusual arrangement. She understood and would receive it as such.

"I would suggest you text me while you are away. I will give you an update whenever asked." Tono scribbled more notes onto the contract. "Toriko, you should be aware that you are expected to contact Sir Davis every Sunday morning to speak for one hour."

Although she knew she should be thrilled contact was allowed, the idea of only speaking to Sir once a week crushed her heart. She felt tears coming, but fought them back.

"There is another stipulation, Brie," Sir added. "I expect you to exercise at exactly six every morning at a local gym minutes from Ren's home. I will be exercising at the same time, only it will be four in the afternoon my time."

Brie felt a sense of relief. Although they would not be talking every day, there would be a daily connection nonetheless. She looked at him and whispered, "Thank you, Sir."

"I assume you have no issues with that?" he asked Tono.

"It seems like a healthy solution," Tono replied with a smirk, "on many levels."

Sir smiled in reaction to Tono's jesting, but it disappeared when he added, "It is important that Brie submits to you fully. I do not believe it is possible to serve two Masters, but I do not want the connection between us to be lost."

Tono put the pen down. "I understand my place, Thane. Temporary Dom. I will treat the role as such." He looked at Brie compassionately.

Sir stood up and held out his hand. "You are an honorable man, Ren."

Tono took his hand and shook it. "Toriko's well-being is equally important to me."

Sir slapped him on the back the way Brie had seen him do with his good friends. "I am counting on it." He picked up the pen and handed it to Tono. "If téa agrees, sign the contract and initial the addendums."

Tono turned to Brie. "Are you willing to become my sub based on these parameters?"

She stood up and bowed to him formally. "Yes, Tono Nosaka."

"Fine, we are all in agreement," Sir announced, sounding as if a big weight had been lifted from his shoulders.

After Tono had signed it, Sir took the contract and added his name and initials before sliding it across the table to Brie.

Brie looked at the pages for the first time. It looked official, like a legal document. Sir handed her the pen, but cautioned, "Read it thoroughly, Brie, before you sign."

She sat back down and read each line meticulously, trying to grasp the concept that she was being transferred to another as she read her Master's wishes in black and white. She hesitated for a moment before finally adding her name to the document, a feeling of apprehension tugging at her heart. She looked up at Sir's confident face and those fears abated.

Brie held out the contract to him. He took the paper and gave her a tender kiss.

Then he turned back to Tono. "I will drop téa off at eight tomorrow morning. She will be packed for the three-week duration. Is there anything you would like her to bring?"

Tono responded immediately with one request. "I would like toriko to bring her favorite vibrator."

She blushed again. Oh, God, what did the next three weeks hold for her?

That night, things were different with Sir. He asked her to lie on the bed, then slowly removed her clothing himself. He caressed her skin as if he were a blind man wanting to 'see' her through touch alone.

She closed her eyes and took in his cherishing contact, wanting to hold onto the feeling so that it would comfort her when he had gone. Brie held back tears, not allowing herself to think about tomorrow.

There was a shift of the bed as Sir settled lower. She gasped and opened her eyes when she felt his tongue between her toes. Brie struggled to stay still as he sensually took a toe in his mouth and sucked lightly.

"Sir…" she whimpered.

"Stay still, little girl."

He moved to the next one, his wet tongue licking in between her toes—the most sensitive area—before taking it into his mouth. She threw her head back and breathed out slowly. It was extremely sexual while being incredibly ticklish—an addictive combination. She moaned when he took her big toe into his mouth. How was it possible that Sir could cause her pussy to contract in pleasure by sucking on her toes?

He moved to the other foot, slowly licking her instep. It made her squirm and struggle.

"Be still."

She instantly stopped her movements and closed her eyes again, her pussy moistening in response to the attention of his mouth.

"Play with yourself," Sir commanded huskily.

Brie slipped her fingers between her legs and started rubbing her slippery clit, craving the extra pleasure. It aroused her to no end knowing that Sir was watching.

His tongue caressed the crease in her smallest toe and she squeaked. He chuckled and nibbled on it lightly as he watched her press her fingers into her pussy.

"Deeper."

She pushed two fingers deep into her vagina and ground against her own hand.

"That's beautiful, téa. You are going to play with yourself until you come." Sir returned to nibbling her toes.

Brie revisited her clit and began flicking it with her fingers enthusiastically. She moaned as his teeth grazed her skin. The first pulse announced her upcoming orgasm. "Sir..."

"Are you close, téa?"

"Yes," she whispered.

"Wait until I bite down."

She nodded, keeping her pussy at the high level of arousal without tipping over. She'd suspected he would make her wait, and he did. But it was glorious to be so deliciously close, to have his attention centered on her.

She opened her eyes and looked up at the ceiling, smiling as she wondered when...

He cradled her foot and turned the sole upward. Brie lifted her head to watch. He met her gaze as he lowered his mouth onto her instep and bit her sensitive skin.

She let out a small gasp as her body exploded in an energetic orgasm. She pressed her fingers against her clit to increase the sensation as her pussy pulsed against her hand.

As soon as it had passed, he released her foot and grinned lustfully. He looked so damn masculine as he crawled between her legs, pushing her thighs apart with his body.

His cock rested at her entrance, but he did not thrust. He gazed down at her instead. "Do you remember the first time I took you as your Master?"

"Of course, Master…" she whispered.

"I plan to take you just as slowly. Feel the depth and width of my love, téa," Sir said as he breached her opening.

Brie held her breath, every fiber of her being concentrated on his shaft. He slid inside a fraction at a time—achingly slow, deliciously arousing—but above all else, the feeling of his love enveloped her.

"I love—" she whispered, unable to finish, the intensity of the feeling choking her.

He looked down as he began to thrust. "I love you, too."

To have not only his dominance expressed, but his love fully communicated in words and actions sent her over the edge. Her spirit floated upward from sheer happiness, and then he took her even further…

"I will always love you, Brie."

He'd used her given name. Brie could not trust herself to speak, but met his every movement, the two becoming one in their emotional dance of souls. When Thane eventually came inside her, she wrapped her legs around his hips and drew him in deeper.

This was her Master. Whoever had control over her, this wonderfully perfect but flawed man owned her heart.

She fell asleep in his arms, no longer dreading what the future held.

Transfer of Power

Brie packed quickly, her hands trembling as she placed the last of her clothing in the suitcase and zipped it closed. Sir grabbed it and nodded to her.

I will miss you… she cried in her head.

Sir had been unusually quiet and curt with her this morning. Neither of them wanted this parting, but Brie dutifully followed him out of the apartment.

The drive to Tono's was silent, but full of unspoken conversations. Would their relationship survive such a test this early on? Brie was suddenly scared again. It was not Tono she feared, but her natural attraction to him. *Will I grow to love Tono too much…?* Brie shook her head, hating her doubts.

"What is it, Brie?" he asked, noting her headshake.

She blanched, ashamed of the reason for her misgivings. "It's nothing, Sir."

He let it drop and stared forward, concentrating on the road.

When they pulled up to Tono's home, Sir turned off the engine and stared at the simple rock garden in the front yard. "We will say our goodbyes now. Once we enter Nosaka's house, I will present you to him, along with the key to your collar."

Brie grasped her collar, shaking her head.

Sir smiled gently, pulling out the key from under his shirt. "The original key remains with me, téa. You are my sub; this arrangement does not change that."

She nodded and wiped away the tear that had formed in the corner of her eye. "I don't want you to go," she whispered, and then looked at her lap, trying hard to keep her emotions in check.

"No tears. Consider this a lesson. Embrace it and learn from it. It is a characteristic of yours that I greatly admire."

"Sir... I am unsure if I am allowed to ask, but I have a personal question about your trip."

"All questions are allowed, even those I may choose not to answer."

Brie voiced a concern that had been burning in her heart ever since he'd announced he was heading back to Russia. Before she lost her nerve, she blurted, "Will you be entertaining Rytsar's subs while you're there?"

His laughter filled the small sports car. "No, téa. This is a business trip. I will have no time for such play." He added in a more serious tone, "I would not damage the newly forged trust between us. This separation will be hard enough without adding that element to the mix."

Brie smiled, letting out a sigh of relief. Of course he would be thoughtful of their growing relationship.

"It is time, téa. Look up and tell your Master good-bye."

She met his confident gaze, but could not stop her bottom lip from trembling. "Goodbye, Master."

He grazed her lip with his finger. "Be my good girl. Follow Nosaka's orders dutifully and with a servant's heart."

"Yes, Master." She could not stop an errant tear from escaping.

Sir wiped away the wetness with his thumb without mentioning it. "I look forward to seeing your completed documentary and hearing about the lessons you learned from Nosaka on my return."

Brie spoke the words that had been pounding in her head, in time with her heartbeat, since she'd woken up that morning. "I will miss you…"

He smiled, but she noticed it did not reach his eyes. "For the first time since my father's death, I am experiencing that emotion as well. I do not care for it, but I assume it is a positive sign."

Brie took his hand and kissed it, choking down her emotions.

His countenance changed to that of a trainer, his voice unemotional and firm. "So now you begin your three-week adventure in the hands of another. Do not burden him with tears. Look at it as the unique opportunity it is."

She accepted that his defensive barrier had reared its ugly head again. "I will, Master."

"The transfer is a formal, but simple ritual. I will present you to Tono Nosaka. You must bow at his feet. When he places his hand on your head, it signifies his acceptance of you as his temporary submissive."

Sir exited the car and walked around to open her door. He pulled her small suitcase from behind the seat and then held out his arm for her to clasp. "Head held high, but at a respectful angle. Chest out."

Those were the same words he'd used the night he'd collared her. She forced herself to smile, even though each step towards the house was killing her inside.

Tono opened the door moments after Sir rang the doorbell. The Asian Dom was dressed in a traditional brown kimono that matched his chocolate-brown eyes. "Welcome, Sir Davis. Won't you both come inside?"

Sir guided Brie ahead of him. "Thank you, Nosaka. I plan to keep this short."

"As you wish," he replied, closing the door behind them.

Tono escorted them into the open living room. Brie vividly remembered the lack of interior walls and the modest décor that spoke of his Japanese background. His home radiated tranquility, helping to calm her nerves.

Brie was disheartened that Sir hadn't been exaggerating about not wasting time. "I present to you my sub, téa." He nodded to her.

Brie instantly knelt at Tono's feet, in an open kneeling position. She closed her eyes when she felt his light touch on her head and had to struggle to hold back a sob in response to the physical transfer of power.

"I accept your sub, téa, for the duration we have agreed upon," Tono answered.

"Here is a key to her collar."

Tono took the small key and closed his hand tightly

around it, bowing to Sir respectfully.

"I leave her in your capable hands, Tono Nosaka."
With that, Sir turned around abruptly and left, without
addressing Brie again. She couldn't believe he was really
gone until she heard the roar of the engine as the Lotus
sped away. The lonely echoes of it could be heard long
afterwards.

"Toriko."

Brie looked up, biting her lip, trying not to cry. He
held out his arms to her.

Brie stood up and accepted his embrace. She closed
her eyes, fighting the feeling of abandonment enveloping
her. To combat it, she concentrated on matching her
breath with Tono's. *This is your life for now…*

His calming voice rumbled from deep inside his
chest. "He needed to leave for his own peace of mind."

She pressed her head against him and nodded meekly
in agreement.

"Are you ready to serve your Master, toriko?"

She broke away and bowed at his feet again, recon-
firming her commitment to him. "It would be my honor,
Tono."

"Remove your shoes and place them at the front
door. Then fill the kettle with water and bring it to me
after it boils."

While she followed his instructions, Tono exited out
of the back door. Brie stood by the stove, not allowing
herself to think. She listened intently to the water
warming in the kettle instead. There was something
soothing about the sounds of the water as it slowly
reached a soft, rolling boil. Waiting gave her time to

adjust to this reality.

Tono was a wise Master.

Master... Brie shook her head in protest, but stopped herself short. Tono had chosen to serve as her Master during Sir's absence. He deserved a willing sub. Sir expected it, and Tono merited no less.

When the water came to a raging boil, she took the teakettle off the stove and joined Tono outside. The sounds of trickling water and birdsong greeted her.

"Good," he replied when he saw Brie. "Place it on the table and sit beside me."

She did as he had asked, kneeling on the small pillow beside him. Brie broke out in a smile when she saw the tea set, the one he had painted with his signature orchid. "I remember this."

He poured the water over the tea leaves to let them steep. "If I recall correctly, you consumed a lot of tea that day."

Brie giggled to herself. "I certainly did. I've never forgotten that lesson, Tono." She paused, then added, "Thank you."

They sat in respectful silence waiting for the tea to steep, the sounds of nature filling in for the lack of conversation. It was...heavenly.

When Tono deemed it ready, he poured the tea and offered her a cup. He said solemnly, "It is an interesting place we find ourselves, isn't it?"

"Yes," she agreed, waiting until he took his first sip before taking hers. She purred when she tasted it. "I forgot how good your tea was, Tono Nosaka."

He smirked. "You and I have similar tastes, little

slave."

It would be so easy to fall into this role with him… She looked deep into his brown eyes and whispered, "To be honest, I'm scared."

He nodded, not seeming surprised by the admission. "This is a precarious role we have been given. To act as partners, but to remain detached."

Is it possible? she wondered to herself. Brie took another sip of the warm liquid, grateful for its soothing effect.

He took a piece of jute from his pocket. "Hold out your left wrist."

She did so, watching with curiosity as he wrapped it several times around her wrist and tied a beautifully intricate knot. "I have the right to remove your collar, but I do not think that would be wise. Instead, I am giving you this." He lifted her wrist to his lips and kissed the knot. "A visual reminder of my mastery over you, but one that does not replace your original commitment."

She lightly touched the jute and smiled. "It is an honor to wear this, Tono Nosaka. Thank you."

He surprised her by grasping her jaw and giving her a kiss. It was a simple, closed-mouthed kiss, but immediately focused her attention on his masculinity.

"I have agreed to refrain from intercourse. However, you should be aware that if I were free to do so, I would ravage you right now on this table." He picked up his cup and sipped his tea slowly. "Understand my feelings. It is with great restraint that I will walk these next three weeks with you."

"Why have you agreed to do this?"

"I find it a worthy challenge. There is no other man who cares for your well-being as much as I do...other than Sir Davis. I could not allow you to flounder alone, or in the hands of a man not suited for you."

"But at what cost?" she asked quietly.

"I love you, toriko. That is my reality. What is imperative to me is that you are safe and able to complete your project. On that score, Sir Davis and I are in complete agreement."

He read the concern on her face and added, "It may be because of my Eastern upbringing, but I accept this role. You and I are connected. Choosing another Master did not alter that fact, although it changed the dynamics between you and me."

Brie took another sip of tea, overcome by the wisdom and compassion of the man beside her. She put her hand over his. 'I am glad to be here...Master."

He grunted and moved his hand away, pouring more tea for them both. "From now on, you will call me simply 'Tono', as you did in the past."

She drained the cup slowly in congenial silence, until a plane flew overhead. She couldn't help but think of Sir and felt a painful ache in her chest.

Tono interrupted her thoughts with instructions. "I want you to go to my bedroom. There you will find the clothes I have set out for you. Wear nothing underneath. You will remain barefoot at all times while in my home. Return to me after you're dressed and present yourself."

Brie rocked off her heels and stood up, bowing to Tono before walking back into his home. She found a red kimono waiting for her on his bed. It was similar in style to the one she had worn for him during the photo shoot, but this one was more modest in length.

She undressed and slipped the silken kimono onto her shoulders. It caressed her skin like a lover's touch, making her smile. On the bed lay a sash. She did her best to wrap it around her waist in an artful manner.

Tono laughed when he saw her. "That's all wrong." He stood up and moved over to Brie, untying the sash. The kimono fell open, exposing her naked flesh. He stared at her appreciatively for several moments before repositioning the kimono and instructing her on how to tie the sash properly. Tono moved behind her and cinched it tight.

She ignored the sexual electricity that sparked from the contact. "Thank you, Tono."

"You will practice tying the sash ten times before bed tonight."

"Yes, Tono."

He went back to the table and sat down, patting the pillow beside him. She joined him as he refreshed their tea and told her to partake. They both put their lips to the cups at the same time. So simple, and yet an intimate act to share with him.

Being here with Tono, caressed by beautiful silk, leisurely drinking tea within the confines of his exquisite garden seemed as natural as breathing.

Revealing Dreams

After tea, Tono instructed Brie to work on her documentary. He followed her into the bedroom, where he had set up a desk for her work station. It looked incongruous with his simple Oriental décor, but it had everything she required to complete the project.

"I wanted you to have the best tools to work with, toriko. I am proud to be a part of your dream, even if it is simply providing you with the environment in which you can produce it."

Brie wrapped her arms around her new Master's waist. "My words cannot express—"

"There is no need. It is my pleasure as your Master. Sit here while I watch your genius."

She smiled bashfully. "The tea has made its presence known, Tono. Let me excuse myself first." When he nodded, she entered the bathroom.

She was about to close the door when Tono ordered, "Leave it open," while he sat down at the desk.

Brie took a deep breath as she mentally accepted the review lesson.

She sat down on the toilet, upright and with all the grace she could muster as her pee trickled into the water. Despite the flush on her skin, Brie appreciated the stripping away of her pride that exposing such a private act to inspection evoked.

He nodded his approval when she came out of the bathroom. "I saw the moment of hesitation, but much more natural the second time, toriko."

"I am still learning, Tono," she responded, suitably humbled.

"As each of us are, little slave. That should never stop."

Brie returned to the desk and uploaded her documentary onto the fancy new computer. "It still needs a lot of work, Tono. This is really a rough draft of sorts…"

Tono chastised her. "Hush. I want to see it without explanations. This is what you presented to the producer, correct?"

"Yes."

"Then that is all I need to know."

Brie knelt down on the floor beside him and the two watched her original movie. Unlike Sir and Mr. Holloway, Tono was full of expression as he watched. He laughed out loud, but looked visibly upset when Brie spoke of Mary's breakdown while in his care.

After the ending credits, he clapped. "I don't care what your producer said—that is a masterpiece." He picked her up and twirled her in the air. "We must go out and celebrate!"

Tono would not let her change, but allowed her to

wear traditional Japanese sandals to dinner. The two went to a local pizza joint, where they stood out like sore thumbs in their Japanese attire. She slid into the seat, quite mindful of the fact she was naked under the kimono. It enhanced the awareness of her own femininity.

She looked across the table at Tono. With or without physical contact, there was an arousing connection between them. It amazed her how Dominants could easily change a normal, everyday experience into something sensual and alluring, even something as innocuous as eating pizza. She bowed slightly when his gaze fell on her.

The hustle and bustle of the place was momentarily forgotten as she stared into his chocolate-brown gaze and received his silent praise.

The waitress scooted over. "Mr. Nosaka, great to see you again! What can I get started for you?"

"I would like you to bring my three favorites, Miss Mallory."

"Three whole pies?" she asked, looking surprised.

"Yes," he answered, with a playful smirk in Brie's direction.

The waitress dutifully wrote down his order, obviously knowing Tono's favorites without asking. "My pleasure, Mr. Nosaka. I'll get Tony started right on those." Her blush and subconscious hair-flip as she walked away from the table let Brie know the girl had a crush on her new Master.

"I came across this place by accident. Best pizza in the world," Tono announced proudly. His enthusiastic claim was that much cuter considering he was wearing a traditional kimono.

Miss Mallory was quick to deliver his requested favorites, but became flustered when she spilled his glass of water while trying to make room for the three pizzas. He gently clasped her wrist, his touch immediately calming the girl. "It's fine. Don't worry about it." He soaked up the water with several napkins and handed them to her with a nod.

The girl smiled appreciatively. "Thank you, Mr. Nosaka." She turned to Brie, acknowledging her for the first time. "He's a good man."

Brie reached over the food and put her hand on Tono's, squeezing lightly. "I know."

The look he gave her was unreadable, but he broke the contact, demanding that she partake.

Brie gladly succumbed to the temptation set before her. Tono hadn't been kidding; it *was* the best pizza she'd ever tasted, with the unusual toppings and brick-fired crust. Her favorite by far was the simple white pizza with spinach, smoked mozzarella and garlic, but she very much enjoyed the sesame chicken with spicy sweet and sour sauce, and the unexpected surprise of the pizza pie with turkey sausage, red onion and pecan.

With Tono's encouragement, she spent the entire meal discussing her film and sharing her plans for additional scenes. She'd never had such a captivated audience before. Tono listened intently, his enthusiasm for her work deliciously contagious. His sincere excitement tickled Brie and gave her hope that she would be a success.

When they had finished their meal, Tono stood up and offered his hand to her. Brie took it, and felt the eyes of the other diners on her. She moved with grace, deliciously aware of her nakedness beneath the thin material. Tono put his arm around her waist and escorted her away from the table, to the envious stares of several women. She felt a thrill of pride as she walked out of the door beside him.

While they strolled back to his place, she laid her head on his shoulder. "I've never had so much fun discussing my work. Thanks, Tono."

He wrapped his arm around her shoulder. "I knew you were good, but I never understood how truly talented you are. This will be a huge hit."

She grinned gleefully. "It helps to hear it. It's easy to doubt yourself, especially when you've put so many hours into it. It all becomes a blur and then you start wondering if you're fooling yourself by thinking any of it is good."

He stopped and physically turned her to face him. "You are no fool. This is a true gem. Do not lose sight of that, toriko, no matter what obstacles are thrown your way."

Tono's confidence had a significant effect on her. He'd infused her with renewed conviction. Even if Mr. Holloway did not bite, she felt certain her documentary would be produced.

"Toriko, I was excited before about your documentary, but now that I have seen it...I am inspired," he said, pressing her body against his in a heartfelt hug. Her body reacted to the contact, wanting to melt into the embrace shamelessly.

Tono pulled away and they continued walking in silence. It was a delicate balance, this act of giving herself to a new Master. Her submissive heart wanted to please him, but she could not dishonor her true Master by giving in to her need.

Part of her wished that she could live two alternate lives—one with Sir and one with the extraordinary man beside her.

That night, Brie made sure to practice tying her sash ten times before undressing for bed. Tono nodded his approval, and then pulled a straw mat from the corner of the room. He rolled it out, then placed a pillow from the bed on the mat and handed her a folded blanket.

"When I was a child I slept on the ground. It is where you will sleep now."

Brie was surprised, but bowed in thanks. "It is my honor, Tono." She dutifully lay on the mat next to his bed, feeling a bit like a pet. But to her surprise, it was not a negative feeling. She curled up in the blanket and closed her eyes in contentment when the lights went out.

She surveyed the room, impressed by the group of people attending. So many beautiful women dressed in colorful gowns, hiding behind decorated masks. She lightly touched the one covering her own eyes, elated to be wearing the color crimson. It marked her as *his*; everyone knew the one to whom she belonged.

Brie was asked to dance by a dashing young man wearing a mask of gold. She accepted his request and they began moving to the old-fashioned waltz. "You are divine," he whispered in her ear.

"Why, thank you," she replied unashamedly as he twirled her.

He handed her a note, and then left her on the dance floor alone. She opened the red envelope and read the words: *Meet your Master in the library.*

Brie kissed it, then fairly skipped off the dance floor, thrilled by his summons. She sauntered down the large hallway and took a deep breath before opening the large wooden door of the library.

The room was dark except for the crackling fire burning brightly on the opposite side of the room. The light of the flames glimmered off the covers of thousands of books lining the walls, and silhouetted the high-backed chairs and the table positioned near the fireplace.

Brie did not see anyone in the room, but shut the door quietly and headed towards the fire, intoxicated by the unknown.

"Stop."

She held herself still, melting at the sound of his voice. Two figures appeared from the shadows—a man wearing a crimson mask, and another with a black mask that complemented his silver hair.

"We are going to play a game, pet."

Brie's heart skipped a beat. His games always proved challenging. "Yes, Master."

The gentleman in the dark mask sat down while her Master moved up behind Brie. His warm breath tickled her neck. "But first, I must undress you."

She felt his hands at the back of her neck as he unzipped her dress and let it pool at her feet. She had been instructed not to wear a bra or panties, so she stood naked except for her high heels before the two men.

"She has lovely breasts," she heard the stranger say.

"That's not all that is lovely about her," her Master answered, slipping his hand between her legs. She felt his middle finger press into her pussy and she moaned softly.

He growled in her ear. "The rules of the game are simple. He watches and directs. You do what he says."

Brie nodded in understanding, goosebumps covering her skin despite the warmth of the fireplace. *What will be asked of me?*

"I want her bound to the table."

Brie looked at the table and noticed for the first time the glint of metal.

"On your back. Put your wrists in the iron restraints," her Master ordered.

Brie had never been bound by hard metal before. She lay down on the table and placed her wrists in the metal cuffs. It positioned her so that her ass lay at the edge of the table. She had to lay her neck on a leather strap screwed into the wood.

Her stomach jumped when her Master locked her first wrist into place. The restraint was unforgiving and hard. The helpless feeling the cold iron evoked was arousing. He locked the other—both were tight enough that she could only wiggle slightly. He moved to her legs next, locking them into place so that her thighs were spread wide and her high heels pressed against her ass. The clank of the metal sealed her fate, making her weak inside.

Then her Master returned to her head and wrapped the leather restraint around her neck. She'd never had a neck restraint before, and it frightened her. He tightened it so that she felt the constant pressure of the leather on her throat and could not move without causing herself discomfort.

Never in her life had she felt more exposed or vulnerable. She whimpered softly, her fears setting in—but not enough for her to call her safe word.

"Is she wet?" the stranger asked.

Her Master leaned forward and felt her pussy with his fingers. He chuckled. "Yes."

"I expected as much."

She watched as her Master undressed and stood beside her, waiting for instructions.

"She would look good in gold."

Brie's eyes followed her Master as he moved to the other end of the table, picked up a golden butt plug and held it up for examination. Brie squirmed as he coated the large tool in lubricant.

He moved out of her line of sight as he bent over to insert it. "Be a good sub and take the entirety of it."

Brie gasped as the tip penetrated her tight hole. It was just like the restraints—solid and challenging.

She was forced to look at the ceiling as he eased it deeper into her ass. The butt plug opened her up and stretched her. She gasped softly, struggling to relax.

Brie's heart was thumping rapidly by the time her

sphincter clamped around the stopper. It was as if a rod had been placed inside, restraining her in yet another way.

She swallowed hard, feeling the leather press uncomfortably against her throat when she did so. It took great will to remain calm.

The older gentleman replied, "Now that she is prepped, I think she needs to be fucked."

Her Master laid his hand on her thigh and trailed his fingers across her skin. "Would you like me to gag her first?"

"No."

Brie felt her pussy gush with wetness as her Master moved into position to take her. She was an object to be enjoyed. Unable to move without discomfort, she was completely at his mercy.

She whimpered when the head of his cock rubbed against her slick outer lips. Despite her fear, despite her distress, she wanted him to use her in front of the stranger. She was desperate for it.

"How easily a goddess becomes a slut," the gentleman observed.

Brie closed her eyes and accepted his words. She was a slut—a slut who needed her Master to dominate her with his cock.

She groaned as he pushed inside her, filling Brie completely. She cried out, needing to pull away, but unable to because of the metal restraints. She was his to do with as he wanted... Only one thing stood in his way—a safe word that she refused to call out.

"Who am I?" he growled, grabbing her thighs and

thrusting with greater force.

"Master!" she screamed.

Her Master took her cry as an invitation and began to fuck her hard. He fucked her like a man possessed. Everything blurred as she fell into his unleashed passion.

"Brie!"

She felt like she was falling into the darkness and flailed about, trying to save herself.

"Brie, wake up!"

She opened her eyes and stopped her struggling when she realized she was in Tono's bedroom. She forced herself to let go of the dream, but echoes of Faelan's domination still lingered over her.

"It's Faelan…" she sobbed, burying her head in the pillow.

Tono lifted his blanket and ordered, "Come to me, toriko."

Brie lifted herself off the floor and slipped under his covers. Tono wrapped his strong arms around her and held her protectively. "It was just a dream."

She shuddered from the intensity of the images and the lustful energy coursing through her. She nestled closer to Tono. "Make it go away," she begged.

"He will no longer haunt you, toriko," he said with finality, and ordered her to go back to sleep.

She lay in his arms and was amazed that the memories of the dream began to slip away as she listened to Tono's even breathing. It wasn't long before she followed him into a deep, restful sleep.

Disclosure

"Brie," Sir called out.

His clear voice demanded attention. She opened her eyes expecting to see him, but quickly realized she was in Tono's bed. She looked at the clock and saw it was five forty-five. She couldn't afford to be late on her first day.

She slid out of the bed, trying not to disturb Tono as she quickly gathered her workout clothes and got dressed. Luckily, the workout center was only a five-minute drive. Sir had arranged her membership, so all she had to do was flash her card to the staff member at the door.

This was her first time working out with the complicated exercise machines. All she'd ever done was lift five-pound weights and jump rope. She found a vacant elliptical machine and attempted to get it to start. After she had pressed many buttons without success, an elderly man took pity on her and instructed her how to use it.

Brie looked at the clock. It was already five after six; she'd missed five minutes with Sir. She started running in place, vowing that she would not be late again. She closed her eyes and called out to him in her mind. *Sir...*

It thrilled her to know that he was on the other side of the world, possibly even using the same equipment while thinking about her. Despite the great distance, she swore she could feel his warm presence surrounding her.

It seemed only natural to tell him about the dream about Faelan as if he were there. She closed her eyes and had a silent, one-sided conversation with Sir. She went on to describe her first day with Tono, and how much fun she'd had discussing the film the night before. *Thank you, Sir. Thank you for asking me to serve under a kind Master while you are gone. I have a better understanding of why you have chosen this for me.*

Brie was sad when the hour was over and she had to say goodbye. She looked up at the ceiling and subtly threw a kiss upwards. "Goodbye, Sir. Until tomorrow."

Upon returning to Tono's home, she was instructed to dress in her kimono and meet him at the dining table. Like the table in the backyard, it was a low-lying piece of furniture with pillows surrounding it. She sat down opposite Tono and smiled. He'd already prepared breakfast for them. It consisted of a mixture of rice, egg and vegetables—not the kind of breakfast food she was used to.

He handed a bowl to her and smiled when he noticed her surprise. "I believe in a hearty Eastern breakfast to start the day. It will give you the energy for all you need to accomplish. Pour the tea, toriko."

She felt self-conscious as she filled his cup, blushing when a drop fell from the spout onto the table. She poured hers next, with no better results.

He said kindly, "I will teach you later."

Brie was grateful, wanting to please Tono as well as learn the proper tea etiquette.

"Today you interview with Marquis. Is that correct?"

"Yes, Tono. I'm nervous about it."

"Have confidence in your purpose and you can overcome any uncertainties."

She reached over and touched his arm. "You are a very wise man."

"Wise, toriko?" He shook his head. "That is reserved for men like my father. I prefer sage-like."

She giggled, his response reminding her of Sir. Brie said in an overly dramatic voice, "Yes, oh sage-like Tono."

He grabbed her wrist and pulled her onto his lap, then pulled up her kimono to smack her naked ass. She squealed when he delivered a firm, stinging slap. He grabbed a handful of her hair and pulled her head back so he could look her in the eye. His eyes sparkled mischievously. "Say it with respect, toriko."

She hadn't expected such treatment from the gentle Dom. Brie responded solemnly, "Yes, my sage-like Tono."

"Better," he replied. He pulled the kimono down and helped her off his lap.

She picked up her bowl of rice and began to eat, attempting to hide the smile on her lips. He certainly was not what she'd expected.

Brie arrived at the Training Center early to make sure she was ready for Marquis' interview. It would not do to keep the trainer waiting, especially when he'd already done so much to help her with this documentary.

She went to the receptionist at the front desk. "Hi. Can you tell me if Marquis Gray has arrived?"

The young woman smiled. "Actually, he has not, Miss Bennett."

"Would it be all right if I—"

"Fancy meeting you here."

Brie's heart nearly stopped at the sound of Faelan's voice. She whispered to the receptionist, "Call Headmaster Coen up immediately."

Faelan sounded genuinely hurt. "Why, Brie? Are you really so cold to me now?"

She turned around slowly, but did not speak.

His blue eyes locked onto hers, so she instantly looked to the floor.

"You have haunted me, blossom. Every waking moment since that damn collaring ceremony."

Brie edged towards the elevator. Unfortunately, Faelan did not take the hint and followed her.

"You haunt my dreams as well."

She gasped, made a beeline for the elevator and mashed the down button several times. The mention of dreams had Brie envisioning the lustful dream encounters she'd had with the Dom.

"I know you still think about me, Brie. I can feel

it…especially at night."

She shook her head violently, staring at the elevator doors, willing Master Coen to show.

"What are you doing, Mr. Wallace?"

Brie breathed a sigh of relief at the welcomed sound of Marquis Gray's voice.

"I came to reschedule our next session and came across Miss Bennett at the front desk."

"Why would you attempt to engage her?"

"I needed to speak with Brie."

"You have been instructed not to, and everything about her posture shouts her discomfort. Take heed."

At that moment, the elevator doors opened to Master Coen's impressive presence. Marquis guided Brie inside. "Take her down, Headmaster. I will join Miss Bennett in a few minutes."

Brie glanced up as the doors closed. Faelan was staring her down, his eyes dark with lust.

"Unfortunate timing," Headmaster Coen stated.

Brie nodded and the two stood in silence until the doors opened to the lower floor.

"I was in a meeting. Go ahead and set up your camera in the room I designated for this interview while you wait for Marquis Gray."

"Thank you, Headmaster," Brie said as she bowed respectfully.

He huffed and headed back down the hallway, mumbling to himself, "This is getting absolutely preposterous."

Brie went directly to the small classroom she'd been given to interview Marquis. She set the camera on the tripod first and then erected her light reflectors, adjusting them several times until she was satisfied. Next, she got out her list of questions and read over them a multitude of times, gradually getting more nervous as time passed.

She waited a full half-hour before Marquis joined her. His stern countenance let her know not to question him about Faelan. "Would you please sit here, Marquis Gray?" she asked, pointing to the seat.

He did so, stating stiffly, "I apologize for the lateness."

Brie smiled, trying to lighten his dark mood. "I truly appreciate you taking the time to meet with me today."

"Let's begin," he instructed, not allowing time for any small talk.

Brie turned on her camera and made a few last-minute adjustments before sitting down next to it, so that it would appear as if Marquis was speaking to the camera when he answered her questions.

"First, I want to thank you for meeting with me today, Marquis Gray."

"My pleasure, Miss Bennett," he replied, without a smile.

She jumped into interviewer mode, not wanting to waste a second of his time. "I am sure many are curious about how one becomes a trainer for the Center."

"It is not something you strive for. The Submissive Training Center looks for individuals who show extensive skill in a particular area. However, they must also have the patience needed to work with students."

"May I ask how you came to work at the Center, then?"

"Headmaster Coen, who was simply a trainer at the time, noted my flogging skills and felt I would be a good match to be on the panel of trainers. I was not interested, until there was an incident with an inexperienced submissive at a club I frequented. I did not witness the abuse myself, but I saw the aftereffects. I regret I was not able to help the young woman, but I determined then that I would make it my mission to empower submissives so that such maltreatment would cease."

"Can you elaborate on the incident, Marquis Gray?"

He raised his eyebrow. "Suffice to say the girl was permanently hurt. That is all I will say about it."

Brie knew better than to push the trainer, and went to her next question. "May I ask how you became a Dominant in the first place?"

"I come from a large family with eleven siblings. I noticed early on that the religious beliefs my parents subscribed to valued appearances more than reality. I could not accept such duality." A slight smile haunted his lips. "Instead, I sought inner enlightenment through pain, similar to the monks of old. Once I'd achieved a sense of self, I desired to help others attain it."

"How old were you?"

His eyes pierced her when he answered. "I was ten."

Brie's jaw dropped, but she quickly recovered. "When did you have your first scene with another person?"

"I was thirteen. The girl was seventeen. She was lost. I aided her in regaining her inner purpose."

Brie had not expected such an answer, and had to think fast on her feet. "How do you feel pain helped her to achieve that?"

"A person's tolerance for pain varies with the individual, but there is a point common to all where pain forces you to focus on the present. Too much pain and that focus is lost. However, if you can maintain the correct level, you can keep a person at a point of awareness that is enlightening. Initially, that was my goal when I started flogging. However, I quickly realized the sexual allure of pain for many. I enjoy delivering both."

Brie's loins trembled—she knew very well the pleasure he was capable of delivering. She cleared her throat self-consciously. "Going back to what you said earlier, you mentioned that your family is religious. Does that mean you believe in God, Marquis Gray?"

He stared straight into her soul. "Yes, I believe in a higher being."

Again, she was stunned by his answer. She'd never considered that practitioners of BDSM would also believe in God. "What religion are you...if I may ask?"

"I do not follow any conventional religion, Miss Bennett. Religions are far too concerned with judgment for me to have any interest."

"I see." Brie was floundering. This was not the direction she'd thought the interview would go. She looked at her sheet and asked the next question on it, realizing how horribly unqualified she was to give such an interview. All she could think was, *Poor Marquis...*

With feigned confidence, she asked, "Marquis Gray, having worked with you personally, I was struck by your ability to...for lack of a better word, read my mind. Is that a skill you have learned due to your exposure with so many subs, or does it come naturally?"

"I do not read minds, Miss Bennett. I discern intent and motivation."

"Have you always been able to do that?"

"Yes."

Brie felt a nervous flutter in her stomach at the thought of Marquis reading people even as a young boy. "That is fascinating. You must have been an interesting child growing up."

Although his expression did not change, she could tell by the way he shifted in his chair that it was not something he wanted to discuss. Mr. Holloway had asked for more intimate details from the subs, but he hadn't said anything about the trainers. It didn't feel appropriate to force the issue.

Moving to something light and generic, she asked, "What is your favorite aspect of being a trainer at the Center?"

"That moment a submissive embraces the totality of what and who they are. Once they reach that level of understanding, they are empowered to live out their lives without compromise."

She was struck by the empathy Marquis had for the students. It was more than simple training; he was truly passionate about improving the lives of the submissives he worked with. She couldn't help wondering if that was the case for all of the trainers. If so, what would she learn about Ms. Clark when she interviewed her the next day?

"So the training that the school provides goes beyond training submissives to master particular tasks?"

"The sole purpose of the Center is to train and educate dedicated submissives so they can realize their full potential. That cannot be achieved by merely learning 'tricks', Miss Bennett. It is a lifetime objective that requires a complete understanding of one's strengths, weaknesses, and personal needs."

She was grateful he had so clearly and eloquently expressed her own experience at the Training Center. "Marquis Gray, I am sure many people are interested to learn what fulfillment you get from flogging a female submissive."

His smile was disarming. She knew women were going to eat it up. "I enjoy the exchange of power, Miss Bennett. Knowing that she trusts me enough to lay down her needs and desires for mine is exhilarating. I also derive pleasure from helping her transform the stimulus I give into something sensuous and beautiful. The connection with her during the scene is unique and cannot be duplicated in any other setting."

The sensations she'd experienced during their many sessions together flooded her mind, and she found herself blushing. Brie fiddled with the equipment to distract herself, hoping he wouldn't notice.

"Turn off the camera, Miss Bennett."

Brie did so immediately, groaning inside. Why was he able to read her thoughts—*no, correct that*—her intent and motivations so easily?

Marquis was not smiling. "This conversation is not meant for public consumption." He moved his chair closer to her before he spoke. "Mr. Wallace is woefully misguided in his conduct, but I understand his motivation. I believe today's encounter necessitates a formal meeting between you two in order to end the unnecessary drama his infatuation is causing. I will speak to both Sir Davis and Tono Nosaka after we finish here."

The idea of meeting with Faelan had Brie spiraling out of control. Marquis gazed into her tortured eyes. "There is no need for concern, Miss Bennett. I am personally mentoring Wallace and have suggested counseling to help him move beyond his past. It is the root of his unhealthy obsession with you. I thought he was further along—however, his behavior today refutes that. It must be confronted."

"Will Sir be at the meeting, Marquis?"

"My opinion is that it should happen sooner rather than later. I believe the connection he has with you can be severed cleanly if done in a timely manner."

"I will only meet with Mr. Wallace if Sir agrees, Marquis Gray. Even if you and Tono punish me for it, I will not without my Master's approval."

Marquis chuckled. "You are feisty but devoted. It pleases me to see it, Miss Bennett. Unfortunately, time is short. This interview is over. However, I was told by Headmaster Coen that you are looking to film a scene with a trainer. I am willing. Did you have a particular submissive in mind?"

Brie's mouth curved into a smile. "If I had my choice, I would choose Lea Taylor."

"I will inform Ms. Taylor after class tonight then. I assume you want to film a session with the flogger?" He gave her an amused look. "Unless you'd prefer her to receive a good caning."

Lucky Lea... Brie wasn't sure she could handle watching a sexy scene between Marquis and Lea without imploding, but she knew that it would serve her documentary well. "A flogging session would be perfect, Marquis Gray. Thank you."

Marquis stood up and shook her hand formally. As he was leaving, he threw out an offhand comment without bothering to look back. "Be sure to bring a towel, Miss Bennett."

When she returned home, the concern on Tono's face alerted her to the fact he had already spoken to Marquis. "I'm questioning if it is necessary to hold your hand wherever you go, toriko."

Brie sighed. "What were the chances *he* would be there?"

"Fate seems determined to bring you two together."

"Why?! It was so uncomfortable, Tono. Faelan wouldn't leave me alone, and when he mentioned the dreams I almost fainted."

"Faelan specifically mentioned them?"

"He accused me of haunting his dreams and said that he knew I was thinking of him because he could feel me at night."

"Did you tell Marquis this?"

Brie looked at him warily, wondering if she had screwed up again. "No. Sir said to always speak to my Master first."

"Fine advice, but Marquis should know, since he is working with the boy. I will mention it to Sir Davis first, before I call Marquis Gray." When he saw her worried expression, he added reassuringly, "You have done nothing wrong, toriko. In fact, based on what I've heard, you handled the entire situation exactly as you should have."

She nodded, grateful to hear his words of praise.

"After I'm finished speaking to them, you will join me and share your impressions of the interview today. In the meantime, boil the pot of water. I will teach you the proper way to pour tea." He pulled away from her and went out of the back door, closing it behind him.

Brie listened to the water boil as Tono spoke on the phone outside. It was difficult to know she could not speak to Sir, but there was comfort in the way Tono was handling the situation. He was respectful of her true Master, but Tono remained in command of her.

With a few words and simple orders, he had her calm and awaiting her first lesson in tea etiquette. He seemed to have the uncanny ability to bring serenity to her soul, no matter the circumstance.

Interviewing the Domme

Brie had gone over her questions for Ms. Clark over and over again. She'd changed them multiple times, only to go back to the original set. Marquis Gray's interview had been so unpredictable that she could not begin to imagine how her interview with Ms. Clark would play out.

It was with trepidation and excitement that she returned to the Submissive Training Center the next day. Thankfully, there were no unexpected confrontations with Faelan to throw her off her game this time.

Brie set up the interview room, then sat pensively waiting for the female trainer—the Domme who had caused her such grief during her six weeks of training. Although Brie had come to respect Ms. Clark, she had never grown to like the woman.

How could she? Ms. Clark hated her guts for no apparent reason.

Which made Brie all the more curious as to why the woman had offered to do this interview. Whatever the motivation, she was going to take full advantage of her time with Ms. Clark. Although Brie was a submissive, she was playing the role of filmmaker now. It allowed her all kinds of latitudes she'd never had with her former trainer.

Like most Dominants, Ms. Clark was punctual. Brie took a deep breath before standing up to shake her hand. "Thank you for coming, Ms. Clark."

"You may call me Mistress tonight."

"Okay…" Already, Ms. Clark was pushing her Dominant role on Brie.

Brie pointed to the chair and adjusted the focus of the camera once the trainer had sat down. Ms. Clark was staring straight at the lens, giving Brie the willies and rattling her confidence.

No, I'm the interviewer! I control this scene…

Brie went straight for the jugular by asking her age. "How old are you, Mistress, and at what age did you realize you were a Dominatrix?"

Ms. Clark looked momentarily shaken but she answered, looking Brie straight in the eye. "I am thirty-two, Miss Bennett. To answer your second question, I understood my role when I was in my freshman year of college."

Brie jumped on her answer. "Was there some incident that caused you to realize that, or had you felt it all your life and simply realized it at this point?"

"I was given the opportunity to top and I found it unusually satisfying. I haven't looked back since."

Brie could sense Ms. Clark was hiding something—there was vulnerability in her eyes that Brie hadn't seen before.

Despite their unpleasant past, Brie had no interest in exploiting that. She switched to a simple question. "How did you become a trainer at the Center?"

"Sir Davis asked me to join the panel. We had known each other in the past and he felt I had the skills and female perspective the Training Center was in need of. You may be interested to know that I was the first female hired to serve on the panel."

That was certainly news to Brie. Sir had personally invited Ms. Clark, a woman he'd known since college, to serve with him at the Training Center? Just how well *did* her Master know Ms. Clark?

"You must be proud of that distinguished accomplishment."

"After my appointment, they made it a policy that a female must be represented on each panel."

As impressive as that sounded, Brie had seen the trainer lose her composure. She did not have the same high regard others seemed to hold for the Domme.

Hoping to uncover the trainer's underlying motivation, she asked the same question she'd asked Marquis Gray. "I'm curious as to why you chose to be part of the Submissive Training Center, Mistress?"

The woman looked at her shrewdly. "The simple fact is I enjoy training new subs. Their untarnished state makes it easier to strip away their egos. It is an entertaining process to see what lies underneath."

Had Ms. Clark's unkind treatment of Brie simply been for training purposes—to strip her bare? No—as much as Brie wanted to believe it, she couldn't. There was more to her harsh treatment than the trainer was letting on. Brie hoped the next question would provoke the Domme to open up.

"Have you ever played the role of a submissive?"

A brief flicker of emotion quickly turned into a hard stare. "I have allowed a Dominant to top me for educational reasons, but I have never been a submissive."

Brie couldn't help thinking, *But I bet you wanted to be, didn't you?* "So Mistress, is it something you would ever consider?"

Ms. Clark tilted her head slightly, narrowing her eyes. "Why do you ask, Miss Bennett?"

Brie felt her skin crawl; her paddling session with the trainer instantly sprang to mind. "I know some Dommes who enjoy reversing roles, Mistress."

"Do not confuse me for a switch, Miss Bennett."

Brie could feel the trainer's defensive walls going up, so she changed the line of questioning accordingly. "What is your tool of choice?"

The Domme answered with an evil curve to her lips. "I favor the cane, Miss Bennett. A good caning can subdue the most errant submissive."

It sounded like a promise...

Brie felt a sudden chill travel down her spine and had to remind herself that Ms. Clark had no power over her anymore. She laughed nervously.

There was no missing the glint in the Domme's eye. What was this interview—a power play?

Brie became outraged at the thought. "Why did you agree to this interview, Mistress?" she asked, point blank, tired of playing games.

The startled look on the trainer's face gave Brie a

feeling of control, boosting her confidence. But Ms. Clark was not about to reveal her true motive, and took several seconds to formulate an acceptable answer. "I believe it is important people understand that Dommes play an important role in the BDSM community. Being a Dominant is not a male-exclusive role, just as being a submissive is not gender-related. It has more to do with a person's character type and his or her sexual desires."

Getting the upper hand gave Brie the courage to voice the one question she had been dying to ask. "Mistress, why do you hate me?"

Ms. Clark gritted her teeth as she pointed to the camera.

Brie turned it off and waited in silence. *Oh, this is going to be good…*

"That is not a professional question. I expected better from you, Miss Bennett. I do not see you lasting long in the film industry."

Brie did not respond, waiting for the question to be answered.

Ms. Clark's voice was cold. "I do not hate you. That would require too much energy and you are certainly not worth that."

Brie ignored the insult, knowing it was a bait and switch tactic. She was not biting.

As the silence dragged on, the trainer snarled. "Your arrogance is not befitting a submissive. I find you immature, selfish and rude."

"So is that why you hate me?"

Ms. Clark snapped, "I said I do not hate you. Let me add obtuse to your list of faults."

"What is the real reason you agreed to this interview, Ms. Clark?"

The Domme growled under her breath. "You are like an itch I must scratch. Everything about you rubs me wrong, and yet…"

The woman did not finish.

"And yet what?"

Ms. Clark stood up, taking off the microphone. "We are done here." She exited the room, leaving Brie alone, completely stunned.

What the hell was that?

Brie packed up her equipment and went to find Lea. She knew the sub was waiting for her, and she *needed* to talk. On her way, Marquis Gray stopped her in the hallway.

"Have you spoken to Ms. Taylor yet?"

"No. I was just on my way to see her now."

"Then it is fortunate I caught you. Tonight looks like the only time our schedules coincide. Can you be set up in an hour in room six?"

"Yes, I can certainly do that. Thank you very much, Marquis Gray."

He nodded. "I look forward to it."

Brie hurried off to find Lea. She found her friend in the sub lounge, sitting on the couch, looking quite pleased with herself. But the instant Lea saw her, she jumped up and gave Brie a huge hug. "Thank you! OMG, when Marquis said he wanted to scene with me, I about died! Thank you, girlfriend!"

Brie hugged her back. "Yeah, I won't lie. When he asked who I wanted him to flog I was tempted to say,

'Me!' But since it can't be me, then I want it to be you."

Lea squealed, "I love having you for a best friend!"

Brie gave her a long, hard squeeze. It was good to see Lea again. "Girl, I had the weirdest interview with Ms. Clark."

Lea grabbed her hand and forced her to sit on the couch. "Tell me about it. I was wondering how it went."

"Well, she was intimidating and rude like she always is with me, but it all changed when I asked her why she hated me."

"You asked her that on camera?"

"Yeah. I've never understood it and I finally just cracked. I *had* to know."

"What did she tell you?"

"She made me turn off the camera before she would answer, but then she gave me the whole 'you're rude and not submissive enough' routine. I pressed her further and she claimed I'm an itch she needs to scratch."

Lea's jaw dropped in disbelief. "She was coming on-to you?"

Brie burst out laughing. "No! I have no idea what she was trying to say. I even asked her, but she just up and left the interview."

"Go back... What exactly did she say?"

"Something like, 'I'm like an itch she must scratch. Everything about me rubs her wrong and yet...'"

"And yet what?"

"I don't know! That's what I asked her and she ended the interview."

Lea shook her head sadly. "Mistress has been extremely aloof since you and Sir returned from Russia. I

231

have no idea what's going on with her."

"It must be something to do with Rytsar; it has to be. Ugh…I hate mysteries! Sir won't let me talk about it, but it's killing me not to know what happened between those three, and why I am somehow caught in the middle of it." She slumped on the couch and whined, "It's not fair…"

Brie understood that Sir did not care for gossip, but was it really gossip when she only wanted to find out about Ms. Clark's past because it was affecting her personally? "Did you hear anything more about Rytsar from Ms. Clark?"

Lea leaned forward, exposing her overflowing bosom to Brie. "Funny you should ask. Right before you left on your trip, she opened up a little about Sir. Whatever mistake she made with Rytsar caused the Russian to go ballistic. His reaction was swift and terrible. Sir stepped in, which is why Mistress holds your Master in such high regard. I have never heard her say anything bad about Sir," she laughed, "other than that he was an idiot to collar you."

Brie hit her friend's shoulder. "I didn't need to hear the last bit, Lea."

"Well, I need to keep you humble. It's my job."

Brie looked up at the clock. "Nuts, I better get things set up for your flogging."

Lea squealed again. "I'm so excited!"

"Well, if you want it to happen, you'd better help."

"I'd do anything for you, Stinky Cheese."

Brie gave her another hug. "Thanks. I really freaked out after Ms. Clark's interview, but now I think I have a better understanding. Unfortunately for me, I am just an innocent bystander who happens to remind Ms. Clark of her past—a past she wishes she could change. Maybe that's what she meant by me being an itch she needs to scratch."

Lea looked at her sadly. "I wish she would just let Rytsar go. There are others who want to love her, but she won't let anyone near her."

Brie shuddered. "I still don't get you, Lea. You can do much better than Ms. Clark, trust me."

"Oh, like you can do better than Sir?"

Brie's laughter filled the room. "Oh, no. I got the best of the best."

Lea pressed her breasts together and tilted her head comically. "And that's why Tono is your Master now?"

Her attempt at a joke stabbed Brie in the heart. She closed her eyes, trying not to cry. "Lea…"

Her best friend instantly apologized, wrapping her arms around Brie. "I'm sorry. That was uncalled for. Please…" She put her forehead against Brie's. "Please forgive me."

She knew Lea hadn't meant to be cruel, but glared at her anyway. "You don't know how close you were to losing that flogging session. I was considering making you a cameraman while *I* enjoyed the pleasure of Marquis."

"Can I make it up to you with a real joke?"

"Absolutely not!"

Sexual Release

B rie focused the lens on Marquis and felt a small thrill when he looked directly at the camera. "Are you ready, Miss Bennett?"

Her loins tingled, even though she was not part of the scene. "I am, Marquis Gray. Act as if I'm not here. I want people to see the intimacy between a Dominant and a submissive. But Lea, whenever you can, verbalize what it feels like for the audience. Oh, and one more thing, Marquis. If it would be okay with you, when you turn on the music, could you keep it low enough that I can hear the thud of the flogger and any exchanges between you two?"

"Very well, Miss Bennett," he answered solemnly. The sound of Mozart filled the room until he turned it down significantly. "Will this do?"

Brie gave him a thumbs up.

Marquis beckoned Lea to him, while still speaking to Brie. "My only requirement is that you do not interrupt the scene once I begin."

"Of course, Marquis."

He turned away from her and ran his hand through Lea's hair. Brie took it as her cue to begin filming. Her body responded as if she were the one receiving his attention.

Marquis ran his hands over Lea's body, lingering at her impressive breasts. "Undress and kneel, facing the far wall. Hands at the back of your neck."

Lea quickly peeled off her clothes and knelt down gracefully. While she was undressing, Marquis took off his shirt and went to the table Brie had set up to pick out a flogger. He grabbed a large black one. "First, we warm the skin."

Lea nodded to signify her understanding.

Marquis swung the flogger slowly in a sideways figure eight pattern, lightly slapping her back with the soothing flogger. Brie knew the feel of it. It looked scary because of its size and many tendrils, but it was made of supple leather that was actually soft to the touch.

The sounds of light thudding and Lea's satisfied sighs filled the small room. Brie's own skin tingled in wistful anticipation. The thuds became louder as he increased the force of impact.

"Color, Lea."

"Green, Marquis. It feels like a warm massage."

The Dom put down the large flogger after several minutes, then picked up one that had fewer tendrils that were also thinner in width. "Now that the skin is warm, I'll increase the sensation."

Brie noticed that Lea's skin was lightly blushed. She did a quick close-up so it would be apparent to the viewer.

When she pulled back, she caught Marquis in graceful motion. He used fluid, solid strokes with the thinner, more challenging flogger. He concentrated on the left side of Lea's back and then moved over to the right, always precise, aiming for the fleshier areas of her skin.

"So beautiful," he murmured under his breath.

Brie saw Lea's muscles stiffen and then eventually relax as her body became accustomed to the more demanding strokes. Her friend's satisfied moans caused Brie to roll her eyes as a trickle of wetness escaped her soaked panties. *I really should have brought a towel...*

When Marquis put down the flogger and turned on the Mozart, Brie's entire body trembled. He returned to Lea with a silk ribbon in his hand. He rubbed it over her bright pink skin, whispering things to Lea that Brie wished she could hear. Her girlfriend turned her head towards him and they kissed. It was long, deep and passionate.

Eventually Brie closed her eyes, still keeping the camera focused on them. Their impassioned kiss was too hot, causing Brie's loins to ache. *Oh, Sir...*

Brie opened her eyes again when she heard Lea cry out. Marquis was using a red flogger this time, the flogger with thin leather tendrils. Brie had not personally experienced their sting, but knew Marquis' natural talent brought a person to the edge without taking them over to the unbearable. Unlike Rytsar, Marquis did not enjoy delivering pain; he enjoyed producing clarity before he sent his submissive into subspace.

Brie melted and the camera slipped for a second. She righted it and held her breath as Lea was taken into glorious subspace.

"Marquis...oh, Marquis," her friend gasped.

The music carried the three of them as he stroked Lea's back with the flogger in time with the music. It was beautiful, sensual, erotic...

Marquis Gray's masculine grace was accentuated by Lea's response to each stroke. Truly, they were poetry in motion. A tear ran down Brie's cheek as she watched. She understood the connection the two were experiencing.

Brie was tempted to slip a finger between her legs, desperate to relieve herself of the sensual ache watching them caused, but she was a professional now. The camera shot was more important than her throbbing need, so she silently suffered for her art.

She watched Lea's back arch. "Give in to it," Marquis encouraged lustfully.

Lea let out a passionate cry as her whole body shook in ecstasy. Brie let out a whimper of her own, swept away by Lea's climax.

Marquis must have heard her, for he glanced in Brie's direction before setting down the flogger and kneeling next to Lea. He wrapped his arms around her and spoke softly, complimenting her body, her sensuality and her spirit.

After several minutes, he helped Lea into his lap and caressed her face as she slowly drifted back to reality. Lea smiled up at Marquis and giggled like a giddy girl. The trainer leaned over, kissing her on the lips. "Charming..."

Brie turned off the camera and closed her eyes, trying

to force her racing heart to slow. How she longed to trade places…but no, that was not true. What she longed for was Sir. She sent out a mental message: *I need you, Sir.*

When Marquis helped Lea off the ground, Brie immediately began putting her equipment away. She needed to get out of there—needed fresh air, and quick.

She jumped when she heard Marquis behind her. "Did you get what you were hoping for, Miss Bennett?"

She didn't dare look at him when she answered. "I got the shots I needed, yes. Thank you, Marquis."

He chuckled under his breath. "I wager you could do with some aftercare."

A shiver ran through her. She said nothing, but her hands refused to cooperate and she dropped her tripod. When he offered to pick it up, she assured him that he'd done enough.

She gave Lea a quick hug. "Sorry, gotta run. Great stuff, Lea. Both of you!"

Brie couldn't get out of the Training Center quickly enough. She found it difficult to concentrate on the roads as she headed home. It wasn't until she saw the valet that she realized she'd headed straight to Sir's apartment. With a groan, she waved the valet away and turned the car around, heading for Tono's.

She burst through the door, dutifully taking her shoes off before collapsing on the floor.

"What's wrong, toriko? Bad day?"

She looked up at Tono in tortured desire. "Help me…"

His countenance changed as he lifted her up and held her close. Brie was certain he could smell her desire. It literally coated her panties.

"I can taste your need," he said, but his voice was not full of lust; it was cool and controlled. "What happened to cause this?"

She sighed. "I had to film Marquis and Lea today. It was…a stimulating scene."

He pulled away and stared into her eyes for several moments before giving directions. "Take a shower and meet me on the mat, unclothed."

Brie felt a twinge of apprehension. What would he ask of her? Would she be able to resist if he crossed the line? In her excited state, she wasn't so sure.

It was with a flood of relief that she stood under the hot, pelting water of the showerhead. It momentarily took away the sexual angst. She reluctantly turned off the shower and dried off in front of the large bathroom mirror. Her honey-colored eyes stared back at her, luminous with need and a touch of fear.

"Toriko…" Tono called from the other room.

The sound of a lone flute floated in the air, letting her know what was about to take place. She took a deep breath before rejoining him. Brie bit her lip when she saw Tono sitting on the mat in his black kimono, with jute in his hand.

She joined him on the mat, kneeling before him. Her stomach jumped when his fingers made contact with her skin. Without asking, he took her wrist and wrapped the jute around it.

"Observe what I do, toriko. I want you to understand the intricacies of the bindings. These are basic, but can still be used for more complicated designs."

Her heart rate sped up as she watched him bind one wrist to the other. He then began a pattern, weaving the rope between each of her fingers, caressing her skin sensually with the jute. She longed to close her eyes and give in to the feeling as she listened to the lone flute call her, but it was not what he had asked of her.

When Tono was done, he held up her hands so she could see the intricate work before he untied it and bound her again so that she could observe it a second time. He left her wrists bound when he was finished, starting on her legs next.

He told her to sit with her ankles together and, using a new rope, proceeded to bind them together. She watched in fascination as he tugged and pulled at the rope, creating tight yet beautiful bonds with simple knots. He untied it, and repeated the procedure for her benefit.

Tono then got up and retrieved something from the bedroom before kneeling behind her. "Breathe with me, toriko."

His words brought a smile to her lips. Brie closed her eyes, embracing the sensual feeling of the bindings as she matched the rhythm of his breaths. He explored her skin with his hands while lightly kissing the back of her neck. "I will bring the release you need," he murmured.

His hands left her momentarily. Brie opened her eyes when she heard the distinctive sound of her little bullet.

She whimpered as he wrapped his arm around her and his fingers made their way between her legs. The instant the little vibrator made contact with her clit, she let out a long and frustrated moan.

"Don't resist," he commanded, pressing it against her.

Brie leaned her head back on his chest. Her nipples became hard with need as the fire began to build inside.

"I desire your orgasm."

She gasped as she allowed the vibration to take her over the edge. Her whole body froze just before the fiery pulsations began. She pushed against Tono as her body released the pent-up sexual energy she'd been suffering from.

"Little slave…" he whispered.

He lifted the bullet from her wet clit, ran it over her stomach and up to her breasts. He tickled her hard nipples with the toy and then returned to the source. Brie stiffened as her clit began dancing with the vibrator a second time.

"I demand another."

She whimpered as her body greedily accepted the challenge. The build-up was slow, but she could tell it was going to be powerful—possibly even painful in its intensity. "Tono…"

"Trust me, toriko."

He helped to build the strength of the orgasm by moving the bullet over her clit, letting the fire burn and then switching the angle so the flow was interrupted momentarily, until he built it up again.

With her hands and legs tied, she was at his mercy—

his wonderful, thrilling mercy. Her legs began shaking first, announcing the impending orgasm. She tried to keep in rhythm with Tono's breathing, but began panting uncontrollably.

"Tono…" she cried.

"Let it consume you, little slave."

That was actually her fear. It felt like the orgasm was about to consume her completely—mind, body and soul. He tightened his grip, pressing Brie hard against him. "Come for me."

The simple bindings, the tightness of Tono's embrace, the relentless vibration of the bullet and her own images of Sir caused a fiery explosion within her core. As it burst forth, she screamed in pleasure and fear. Brie struggled against Tono as it swept through her. The power of the orgasm obliterated everything, almost claiming her consciousness before it ended.

She groaned in satisfaction, her body tingling long after her release. Brie opened her eyes, her body and mind finally free from the desperate need that had eaten at her. She took a deep breath and turned her head to smile at Tono. "Thank you, Master of the Rope."

"It was not just for you, toriko. I was confronted by your need the minute you entered the house. Without immediate intervention, I would have fulfilled it in a manner outside the bounds of the agreement."

"I shouldn't have agreed to film Marquis. I was just asking for it…" she said, rolling her eyes at her own foolishness.

"Knowing your attraction for flogging, I would have to agree," Tono answered with a smirk as he began slowly untying the knots.

When he was finished, she asked, "Would you allow me to practice on you?"

He hesitated for a moment, but handed over the rope. "Let me see what you've learned."

Ties that Bind

Brie took the cord and folded it in two. She wrapped it around his wrists, pulling the rope through the loop in the middle. She looked up at Tono and smiled as she pulled it tight. She wound it around his wrist several times and looped it under before starting between his fingers.

Brie laughed when she was done. The knots were different sizes, his fingers spread far apart and the ends dangled unattractively. Still…he was bound and she found it surprisingly sexy.

She lifted his hands up and gently, but forcibly, pressed her body against him so that he lay down on the mat with her on top. Brie felt his rigid cock against her stomach. Obviously he found it as erotic as she did.

It seemed a shame that she had enjoyed an earthshattering release, but he had been denied his. Brie opened his kimono so that his shaft rubbed against her naked skin. Still holding his arms, she whispered, "Don't move."

Brie rubbed her abdomen against his hard cock,

rocking her hips sensuously. Tono shook his head, but did not resist. She moved against him, increasing the pressure between them. She felt the wetness of his pre-come and moaned, knowing that she was bringing him close. She was drawn to his lips…

Tono gave a deep-throated groan when she kissed him, his manhood spasming between them, but he refused to come. He suddenly brought his bound wrists down around her, capturing her in his embrace. "Do not do that again."

Although he said it without malice, she wondered at his words. Was he displeased with her?

"Untie me," Tono insisted after releasing her from his embrace. She fumbled with the poorly formed knots. It took extra time to set him free because of her amateur attempt.

Once free, he stood up. "Stay." He left her and retreated to the bedroom. He returned with an armful of rope and the silver ring he used for suspension. She shivered in anticipation.

"This will be demanding on you, toriko. The bindings and pose will challenge your body."

Her heart sped up, but there was no way she would turn down such an opportunity. "I long to be challenged, Tono."

He sat down on the mat and laid out the long lengths of jute beside him. He motioned her to him. "Kneel, facing away from me."

She did as she was asked, her whole body buzzing with excitement. Tono started with her chest, binding it tightly, framing her breasts with the rope. The subtle touches as he pulled and adjusted the rope were hypnotically sensual. This time there was no music, just the slap of the ends of the rope as they smacked the floor with each pass.

He bound her arms one at a time, covering them in a decorative three-inch diamond pattern. He moved down to her abdomen, attaching a rope from her chest as he bound it in the same ornamental pattern.

She gasped softly when he reached between her legs and pulled the rope taut against her clit and up the valley of her ass. He fastened it in the back, pulling it even tighter before tying the final knot. The pressure was arousing, causing her body to react.

"Tono, I've wet the jute."

He chuckled under his breath. "To be expected, little slave."

He continued down her legs with the diamond pattern. The bindings were tighter than normal, but not challenging. When he had tied off the rope at her left ankle, he told her to lie on her stomach. While she followed his orders, he began fastening the silver ring to the ceiling. He tested it out with his full weight before returning to her.

He pulled her arms back and secured them so that she felt like a swan in mid-flight. Tono lightly caressed her back and thighs before taking her right ankle. He pulled it backward towards her wrist. She lifted her chest off the ground to accommodate the position as he secured her ankle to her wrist. Brie imagined she looked like a dancer with her arms thrown back and a leg gracefully kicking backwards.

He made it even more challenging when he finished the pose by binding her left ankle to her other wrist. Tono was right. It was a demanding pose, and she hadn't even been lifted off the ground yet. It was unpleasant to have her body weight centered on her torso and chest.

He ran his hands over her skin again, soothing her with his touch. "Breathe with me, toriko," he gently reminded. Brie concentrated on matching his breath, staving off the discomfort. He quickly bound the rope at several points and slipped it through the ring. "And now you fly."

He began slowly lifting Brie off the ground. Instantly, the jute began to tighten and dig into her skin. The tightness around her chest was more acute than before, but there was also a sexual pressure added with the rope resting on her clit.

"Breathe with me," he reminded her again.

She closed her eyes and forced her body to accept the challenge of the jute. Once Tono had her lifted and secured, his hands returned to her, caressing her skin as he made minor adjustments to the rope.

"As Dom, I am the one in control, little slave."

"Yes, Tono," she said as she slowly twisted in the air. She wondered if he was talking about her grinding against his cock.

"What you did provoked me, toriko."

She looked up at him, unable to tell if he was joking or not. "Tono, I wasn't trying—"

"I do not care to be topped." He reached over and slapped her ass with a biting smack. She squeaked, surprised by his move and slightly turned on by it as she swung back and forth from the force of the swat.

Brie squirmed and whimpered as he continued to slap her ass cheeks, making them warm with his punishment. She'd never known the sexual allure of being spanked for misbehavior. It felt like a guilty pleasure, one she knew she should not enjoy, but her wetness exposed her true sentiments.

Tono paused and she thought he was done, but then his hand landed on her warm buttocks again. The tingling feeling on her skin moved straight to her pussy. The next swat really hurt. Brie cried out in alarm. It hurt—oh, God, it hurt—but it was so damn sexy coming from her gentle Master.

"No more topping."

"No, Tono, no more topping."

"Now that you have been punished, I will take my pleasure."

Tono left her side to rummage through an ottoman that also acted as extra storage. He pulled out a plastic mat and laid it under her before picking up a long, red candle and lighting it in front of her.

Brie whimpered in pleasure as he dripped some of the hot wax on her tingling buttocks. He slowly moved up her back. She groaned as the wax made thin trails on her skin. He moved to her front and slipped the candle into a tight loop he had created previously with the rope.

Tono grabbed Brie's chin roughly and kissed her as melted wax dripped onto her shoulders. Her pussy pulsed against the jute and she moaned loudly.

He untied his kimono and moved behind her. Brie's loins contracted in anticipation. Tono ran his hands over her body, caressing the skin, sliding them over the rope until his fingers rested on the slick jute binding her pussy.

He put one hand on her ass. Although she could not see his actions, she knew what he was doing because of his jerking movements and low grunts. Knowing Tono was masturbating on her was an incredible turn-on.

Another drip of burning wax hit her shoulders just as he groaned and hot liquid covered her ass and pussy.

"Yes, Tono, yes…" she moaned.

After he was done he pushed on her thigh, causing her to twist around slowly on the rope. Brie closed her eyes and took in the extreme sensations of constricting jute, the pull of gravity, hot wax, warm semen and flying…

She heard the clicking of a shutter and opened her eyes to see Tono taking photos of her. She managed a slight smile before she closed her eyes, moving towards the promise of spiritual flight, but Tono pulled her back.

"No, toriko." He stopped her spinning, blew out the candle, and lowered her to the floor. She wondered if this was another aspect of her punishment, but as he untied her he explained, "It is not safe to stay suspended in that pose for long."

The deep indentations the rope had left began to burn as the blood rushed back into her skin. Tono eased it by rubbing her down, forcing the blood to return quickly. He laid her across his lap afterwards and meticulously removed the wax from her skin, allowing Brie to bask in the afterglow of the experience.

When he was done, he asked Brie to join him in the

shower.

She followed Tono into the bedroom and watched as he shed his kimono, his toned body causing an instant reaction. As he walked into the bathroom, she couldn't help appreciating his firm ass. Why did he have to be so beautiful?

Brie reminded herself that the Training Center had specifically chosen this Dom for her because he was the embodiment of her top attributes in a man. It was no wonder she was physically attracted to him.

Tono handed her the bar of soap. It slipped out of her hand and she was forced to pick it up from between his legs. Her gaze took in his handsome stature as she slowly stood back up. To calm her unwanted attraction, she turned away and concentrated on replaying the procedure for binding in her mind while she soaped up.

He exited the shower first, as she was rinsing off. She stepped out a few seconds later to find Tono drying his wet hair with a towel. It seemed so natural and cute, as if they'd been a couple for years.

"Join me in bed when you are dry, toriko," he said as he tossed the towel on the counter, then left the bathroom.

Brie wondered what he had in mind. She quickly dried off, then slipped into bed with him. Tono pulled her close, causing nervous butterflies in her stomach. When she felt his warm breath against her neck, Brie was certain she knew where the night was heading, and wondered if she would be forced to use her safe word.

She couldn't have been further from the truth.

Tono's voice was grave as he spoke. "I told you once

that my father does not share the same connection with my mother that you and I have experienced."

Brie shivered as if cold water had been splashed on her at the change in his tone, and only nodded in response.

"My mother is overbearing, incapable of submitting her will."

Brie stared at the wall and admitted her confusion. "I don't understand, Tono."

"Although my father is a Master in the community, he is not Master in his own home."

She closed her eyes, worried about the answer to her next question. "What does it have to do with us?"

"What you did, although enjoyable, still angered me."

She turned and gazed into his chocolate eyes. "Tono, I didn't mean to top you."

"I understand your heart, toriko, but anything that even hints to it rubs me the wrong way."

"But you didn't stop me," she protested quietly.

"I was controlled by desire," he replied, stroking her cheek lightly. "Which is something else I do not care for."

It upset her to have displeased her Master. "I am genuinely sorry, Tono. I never—"

He silenced Brie by kissing her on the lips. "We each have our own triggers, toriko. Now you know mine..."

Master's Voice

B rie anxiously awaited her first conversation with Sir. Tono suggested that she take the call in the backyard garden, where she would have not only privacy, but peaceful surroundings. On the outdoor table were two items—her cell phone and a small gift box. Her curiosity was piqued.

She stared at the phone, knowing that Sir would call exactly on time but hoping against hope he would break protocol, just once. Precisely at eight, the phone rang.

She answered it without allowing another ring. "Sir?"

"Brie."

A flood of warmth moved through her at the sound of his voice. "I've missed you, I've missed you so much, Sir!" She had to hold back the tears that threatened to break her.

"Are you well?" he asked.

"I'm so much better now. I love hearing your voice." The sound of his laughter tickled her beyond measure, and she pressed the phone against her ear, not wanting to miss a word.

"I am equally pleased to hear your voice, my little sub. Are you serving your new Master well?"

After last night's misstep, she was unsure how to respond. "I'm doing my best, Sir."

"It is all I ask. I'm sure Nosaka will fill me in if there are any issues that need my attention. Have you had any more dreams or encounters with Mr. Wallace since I last talked with Tono?"

"No, Sir."

"Any other issues that are concerning you?"

There was only one she wanted to express. "I miss you."

Brie longed to hear how much he missed her, that he was coming home because of it. Instead, Sir responded, "But you are well, and you are getting your filming complete?"

"Yes, Sir," she answered obediently. Brie was desperate to hear his voice rather than her own, so she asked, "Is work going well? Are you making good progress?"

"There is adequate progress being made." He switched the line of questioning back to her. "Do you feel you will be able to make the deadline for the documentary?"

"Yes, Sir. Tomorrow, I'll be editing the interviews I did the last couple of days. I am making adequate progress, too."

"Good. Your success is as important to me as my own."

"As is yours to me, Sir."

"Have you been my good girl and exercised every day?"

"Of course, Sir! It's my favorite way to start the day."

His warm laughter thrilled her. "I look forward to it as well. However, I desire a deeper connection. I want to bring structure to our daily encounter."

Brie was intrigued. "I would like that very much as well, Sir."

"There should be a package near you."

She smiled. "There is, Sir."

"Put the phone down and lift the lid. Read the note to me."

She slowly untied the bow and lifted the lid of the pretty box. Inside was a small envelope on top of a piece of jewelry. She opened the envelope and pulled out the note, then picked up the phone to read his words. "*Wear this each morning while you exercise.*"

"Good girl. Now describe the jewelry to me."

Brie put down the note and picked up the unusual blue and gold piece with one hand, while she held the phone to her ear with the other. "It's beautiful, but it's nothing like I have ever seen. The three-inch glass is cobalt in color and curved like a finger, but it's thicker on one end. It's rounded and smooth with a gold decoration attached to one side of the glass. The gold has a pretty filigree design etched in it. Instead of being attached to a chain, the thin elastic material looks suspiciously like a thong, Sir."

"If that is true, Brie, where would the jewelry go?" he asked.

As she examined the piece, it dawned on her that the glass was meant to be inserted into her vagina so that the gold decoration covered her clit. "Is this pussy jewelry,

Sir?"

"You could call it that," he said with amusement.

Brie's loins moistened at the thought of inserting the rounded glass into her vagina. What would it feel like? What would it look like? She couldn't wait to try it on and find out.

"Tomorrow morning, wear the jewelry and think of your Master."

"Sir, I won't be able to think of anything else!"

"I will be thinking of you wearing it as we exercise together," he said lustfully.

Brie shivered at the thought. "I can't wait for tomorrow, Sir." With his gift and simple command, he had completely changed the experience of her morning routine.

"There is one more thing in the box, Brie, but I don't want you to open it until our conversation is over."

She tingled with excitement at knowing there was another surprise. "May I *please* open it now?"

His answer was emphatic. "No."

She didn't waste time begging. "Thank you in advance, Sir. I can't express how touched I am by your gifts." She played with the bow on the box. His thoughtfulness was proof he was missing her. He might not have said it in words, but this was more than enough.

Their time on the phone ended far too quickly. Before she knew it, she was listening to Sir saying goodbye. Then the buzz of a dead line took over. She struggled to hold the tears at bay as she picked up the box and looked for his final gift, but she didn't see anything. Brie lifted up the satin lining and found another note, written in

Sir's elegant handwriting.

She took it from the box with trembling fingers, knowing it must be important.

In the cold Russian snow, a flower catches my eye.
Breaking through the icy shards
In the sea of white, its radiance springs hope.
Its tenacity stirs a hardened heart,
Adding to its allure.
It is a strength to be admired
A miracle to behold.
Delicate, with the heart of a warrior
Rare in its beauty
Priceless in its worth.

Everywhere I look, I see this tiny flower blooming in
the snow and am reminded of you.
~Love, Thane

Warm tears threatened to fall on his poem. She wiped them away, crushing the note to her chest. The romance of a poem and the love expressed in his words filled her heart with a level of peace she'd never known. She sat there, completely entranced by it.

Everything she'd experienced took on a different meaning. The realization that time and distance had no effect on the strength of their love was powerful, life changing. Nothing could prevent it from growing deeper—nothing.

Brie experienced a significant paradigm shift in that moment. With renewed conviction, she stood up and entered Tono's home. She walked over to Tono, greeting him with a bow.

"A good conversation?" he asked.

"Very good, Tono."

Looking at the box in her hand, he explained, "Your gift arrived yesterday, but I was instructed to wait until the phone call to give it to you."

A deep, overflowing love for Tono filled Brie's heart. Not the romantic love she had felt for him prior to now, but the deep-seated love of a kindred spirit. "Tono, I want you to know how honored I am to be your submissive." She bowed low at his feet.

"I accept your gratitude, toriko, but must ask what has brought this sudden need to express it."

She looked up at him with tears in her eyes. "I finally understand... I cannot love you as a mate, but the intensity of my love for you has not changed."

He nodded and indicated they sit down. "Love can be redirected, toriko. Given time, the sexual attraction will dissipate as we move forward with our lives. But to deny the feelings we have would be foolish and unnecessary."

She smiled and held out her hand to him. He took it and squeezed gently. "I ask again, what brought you to this conclusion?"

"Something Sir did today brought me deep inner peace. No time, distance, or personal struggles can separate us. I believe that to my very core. With that realization, I can now accept my love for you. Ever since my decision at the ceremony, I have seen that love as a threat to my relationship with Sir, but now I understand it is not."

"No, it is not, toriko. As a man of principles, I would never allow myself to come between you. But I will admit that being with you in this capacity has been enlightening."

She looked at him warily, afraid Tono would say that she had failed him.

He laughed. "You believe you have disappointed me?"

Brie looked to the floor. "I *know* I have, Tono. Have you forgotten last night?"

He waved it off. "That was minor, toriko. No, I am speaking of the routine and comfort of a mate that I have experienced with you. I am no longer satisfied with the solitary life I lead." Brie felt a twinge of guilt. This would have been his life, had she chosen differently. He continued, "I am now consciously listening for the soul call of my partner."

Brie was thrilled to hear it. "Whoever she is, Tono, she will be worthy of your love. You deserve only the best."

He looked away from her. Instead of responding, Tono changed the subject. "Tomorrow we have our first class together. How do you feel?"

She answered, accepting the change of topic without question. "If I only have to accept your bindings, I will have no troubles."

"Even with an audience of amateurs?"

"I won't even notice," she said with a small grin.

"You have that effect on me."

"True," he agreed with amusement.

"How may I serve you today, Tono?"

"Due to tomorrow night's class, I want you to spend the entire day working on your film. As you can't cook and I can't spare the time, I will order in our meals. While you work on the documentary, I'll prepare my notes for the class and go over them with you tomorrow before the session."

"It sounds like the perfect plan."

He banged his fist on the table for dramatic effect. "Make it so, little slave."

Brie got up from the table but paused, looking back at him shyly. "May I hug you, Tono?"

A warm smile spread across his face. "Yes, toriko."

She moved into his open arms and closed her eyes as he enfolded her in his manly embrace. "Can I tell you that I love you, Tono?"

"Yes."

"I love you, Tono Nosaka."

He rested his chin on the top of her head. "I love you too, toriko. That will never change."

Something evil is waiting in the wings…

Discover what has the power to tear Brie's world apart in *Protect Me*.

Buy the next in the series:

#1 (Teach Me)

#2 (Love Me)

#3 (Catch Me)

#4 (Try Me)

#5 (Protect Me)

#6 (Hold Me)

Brie's Submission series:

Teach Me #1

Love Me #2

Catch Me #3

Try Me #4

Protect Me #5

Hold Me #6

Surprise Me #7

Trust Me #8

Claim Me #9

You can find Red on:
Twitter: @redphoenix69
Website: RedPhoenix69.com
Facebook: RedPhoenix69

**Keep up to date with the newest release of Brie by signing up for Red Phoenix's newsletter:
redphoenix69.com/newsletter-signup**

Red Phoenix is the author of:

Blissfully Undone
* Available in eBook and paperback
(Snowy Fun—Two people find themselves snowbound in a cabin where hidden love can flourish, taking one couple on a sensual journey into ménage à trois)

His Scottish Pet: Dom of the Ages
* Available in eBook and paperback
Audio Book: *His Scottish Pet: Dom of the Ages*
(Scottish Dom—A sexy Dom escapes to Scotland in the late 1400s. He encounters a waif who has the potential to free him from his tragic curse)

The Erotic Love Story of Amy and Troy
* Available in eBook and paperback
(Sexual Adventures—True love reigns, but fate continually throws Troy and Amy into the arms of others)

eBooks

Varick: The Reckoning

(Savory Vampire—A dark, sexy vampire story. The hero navigates the dangerous world he has been thrust into with lusty passion and a pure heart)

Keeper of the Wolf Clan (Keeper of Wolves, #1)

(Sexual Secrets—A virginal werewolf must act as the clan's mysterious Keeper)

The Keeper Finds Her Mate (Keeper of Wolves, #2)

(Second Chances—A young she-wolf must choose between old ties or new beginnings)

The Keeper Unites the Alphas (Keeper of Wolves, #3)

(Serious Consequences—The young she-wolf is captured by the rival clan)

Boxed Set: Keeper of Wolves Series (Books 1-3)

(Surprising Secrets—A secret so shocking it will rock Layla's world. The young she-wolf is put in a position of being able to save her werewolf clan or becoming the reason for its destruction)

Socrates Inspires Cherry to Blossom

(Satisfying Surrender—a mature and curvaceous woman becomes fascinated by an online Dom who has much to teach her)

By the Light of the Scottish Moon

(Saving Love—Two lost souls, the Moon, a werewolf and a death wish...)

In 9 Days

(Sweet Romance—A young girl falls in love with the new student, nicknamed 'the Freak')

9 Days and Counting

(Sacrificial Love—The sequel to In 9 Days delves into the emotional reunion of two longtime lovers)

And Then He Saved Me

(Saving Tenderness—When a young girl tries to kill herself, a man of great character intervenes with a love that heals)

Play With Me at Noon

(Seeking Fulfillment—A desperate wife lives out her fantasies by taking five different men in five days)

Connect with Red on Substance B

Substance B is a platform for independent authors to directly connect with their readers. Please visit Red's Substance B page where you can:

- Sign up for Red's newsletter
- Send a message to Red
- See all platforms where Red's books are sold

Visit Substance B today to learn more about your favorite independent authors.